She had to laugh because his grin was very engaging. And really, he had the most incredible eyes. The carrying her up the stairs was kind of a romantic touch, but she wasn't sure she wanted romantic. Hot, sweaty and wild, absolutely.

Romance was optional.

"First door on the left."

The door to her bedroom was almost shut.

Open only one telling inch.

*What?*

Reign's body froze. Her son wasn't home, and she sure as hell knew she hadn't left that door closed, and the alarm was off. "Put me down."

At that moment she was glad Nick was everything she suspected he might be because he dropped her on her feet, and drew a weapon from behind his back with what looked like fairly impressive precision. The gun fit his hand naturally and he was comfortable with it. That didn't surprise her at all somehow.

"We got a problem here?" he asked her, slanting a razor-sharp glance her way, but she knew his attention was on that almost-shut door.

Reign said a prayer of thanks Vince was far away and nodded. "I think so."

# Renee Graziano

# PLAYING
*with*
# FIRE

A TOM DOHERTY ASSOCIATES BOOK • NEW YORK

This is a work of fiction. All of the characters, organizations, and events portrayed in this novel are either products of the author's imagination or are used fictitiously.

PLAYING WITH FIRE

A Tor Book
Published by Tom Doherty Associates, LLC
175 Fifth Avenue
New York, NY 10010

www.tor-forge.com

Tor® is a registered trademark of Tom Doherty Associates, LLC.

ISBN 978-0-7653-8350-1

Our books may be purchased in bulk for promotional, educational, or business use. Please contact your local bookseller or the Macmillan Corporate and Premium Sales Department at (800) 221-7945, extension 5442, or by e-mail at MacmillanSpecialMarkets@macmillan .com.

First Edition: April 2014
First Mass Market Edition: November 2015

Printed in the United States of America

0  9  8  7  6  5  4  3  2  1

## Dedication and Acknowledgments

First and always first I'd like to thank GOD ... not just for getting me where I am today but for making me walk through the fire in order to know how to PLAY WITH FIRE.

To my sister Jennifer: Thank you, thank you, thank you ... for never giving up on me and for never failing to see my potential through all the drama. You have pushed me to limits I didn't even know I was capable of reaching. You have taught me to explore roads I have never traveled, come to terms with things I never wanted to ... and be above the rest without acting like I am above the rest.

Daddy: You are without a doubt the greatest man I know. You have taught me courage, perseverance, and forgiveness. You have showed me that your presence in a room isn't weighed by how much you are feared or how loud you are but by the amount of kisses on your cheek and handshakes or just your plain old ability to make others laugh.

Mom: You are a driving force in my life. Also a

bit of a pain in the ass, but without you I wouldn't know what style, beauty, and grace are. Without you I wouldn't know how to love unconditionally nor would I know how to say screw what people say. . . . It's all about family!

Lana: What can I say? We've been through everything that two sisters could go through in ten lifetimes . . . marriage, divorce, pain, pressure, and single parenting. I love you.

Justin, Sonni, John, and Anthony: TiTi Nae loves you!!!!!

Monica Cooper: You held me together when I couldn't keep it together. . . . You were always there to lend a helping hand and a comforting phone call when I needed it. You have the patience of a saint. Xoxo

Marvin Peart: You do not know how grateful I am for not getting up when I was sitting at your table in Spa!! Ha-ha! That was the beginning to a friendship I hold so near and dear to my heart. By the way, you sure do know how to spot a star when you see one, and I am not talking about me, I'm talking about my sister Jenn.

Alexis, Marilyn, and the sassy Ms. Margo: Where would I be without you three?!!!! Alexis, you're more than my cousin to me, you're my sister. I love you so very much!!! Marilyn, you are a second mother and someone I admire tremendously. Margo, the coolest most calm and collected Gemini I know!!!!! Hats off to a woman who remained in charge!!!

Tiffany Hasbourne: You played a major role in

my life and if I've never said it before or a hundred times, here's the first and the one hundred and first time: THANK YOU!!! AppreciatCha!!! Xoxo

Danielle, LyMarie, and Bali: You girls are a rare find, a precious gem and I'm honored and so grateful to have you as my friends.

Nikki Boots: This book was great therapy!! Write one!! Or date more, lol. . . .

My Prude Prude: . . . It's not a bad thing. It's a boring thing. Hahahahah.

Carla Murino: You have been there with me through hell and back from third grade to today. We've argued and possibly had a fight or two. We laughed, cried, and have been each other's alibi!! #bff #pastels #tebf #stitches #prisonvisits #stmichaelschurch #pontessteakout #fromthebasement #tothetop #mobcandy.

Aunt Celia, Bianca, Andrea, Aunt Belinda!!! I wish you were here so I could share this triumphant moment with you!!!!

My cousin Erica and Frankie.

Aunt Patricia Dana.

To my grandmother Nora!! All I can hear is your voice as you fought with your sister, Ti Suzie, screaming BouTana back and forth in your Italian accents!!!!! Oh man, do I wish I could have one more day with you on earth. I think about you daily and I know you are watching over me!!!

Grandpa Anthony: I used to run to greet you at the door and fall down the steps every time because I was so excited to see you. You never, ever missed my birthday right up until the year you died. Twenty bucks for twenty-four years.

Grandpa Sal: You were definitely no pushover, but I remember you taking me to pick daisies and blackberries.

Grandma Faye: Heaven is a place of harmony. Don't be stirring up some shit. . . . Just joking. Please watch over your son, my father, and keep him safe and alive till he's 101.

Uncle Sal: You taught me how to fish and as you can tell I still haven't caught one—hahah.

Grandmother Kitty.

Aunt Sally, Aunt A, Aunt Mary!!

My cousins Susan (rest with angels) and Kathy: Living with you guys will always be a fond memory.

My Great Aunt Prudy: The real deal Playboy bunny!!

Dena and Angie.

Grace Ann Vacarro: My friend on earth and my angel in heaven. I miss you terribly!!!

Jo Mignano: I thank grace every day for you, you are an incredible friend and one hell of a P.R.

Nikki Boots: #acbound.

Andrea: From bowling to Waldbaum's parking lots to the end of time I love and miss having you in my life. Don't let your daughter read this!! And give your mother and sister a kiss. xoxo

Mrs. Murino.

Suzanne Corso and her mom, Judy: I remember sitting on your bed and you reading me pages from your book before we were nineteen. We did it!!!!!!!!!

As for the men in my life . . . though I've dated

more than the average and less than some, I can honestly say there were only a few good men . . . and maybe three greats!!!

You know who you are. Won't catch me telling . . . cause that would be snitching and THAT'S NOT THE WAY I GET DOWN.

And last but so far from least; the BEST AND MOST IMPORTANT IN MY LIFE:

My son! AJ!!! Mommy loves you more than life. You are my child, my best friend, and my savior on Earth . . . let alone one of the wisest young men on the planet with the most beautiful heart and soul. Because of you the world is a better place. Your mom did it, buddy!!!! I hope you are proud of me!!!!

A special thanks to the publishers, editors, and the strong, sexy bold women behind this book. A special nod to my agent, Brandi Bowles of Foundry Media; Barbara Poelle of the Irene Goodman Agency; and my fabulous editor, Kristin Sevick. Also to the unsung heroes: the art department, the copy editors, and proofreaders at Tor/Forge.

Transitions Recovery Program!! One Day at a Time.

To the rest of my family and friends: I love you for believing in me!! I love you for loving me. I love you for supporting me and I love you even more for letting me be without judging me.

# PLAYING
*with*
# FIRE

# PROLOGUE

The pool shimmered Caribbean blue under the moonlight, and the slight splash was the only sound she could hear over the accelerated respiration of her own breathing.

Reign slid her hands over the shoulders of the man who held her. Their bodies were slick in the water, her legs around his waist, his hands cupping her hips, holding her in just the right position as his lower body moved urgently. . . .

"Baby," he said on a suffocated breath, his breath hot in her ear. "Holy fuck . . . tell me you're close. This is too good. I can't hold on."

She was close. Aroused, immersed in sensation, the light slap of the water as they moved together part of the moment. Her arms wound around his neck. Her breasts were tight against his muscular chest, and then the world shattered and went away as her orgasm rose, crested, and spilled over. The

*tidal wave was all heated sensation and perfect plea-*
*sure as she washed away in the flood.*

*She floated, literally, into reality, the face of the*
*man still holding her indistinct in the shadowed*
*light, and she smiled and lifted a wet hand to touch*
*his mouth.*

*"Hmm. That was . . ."*

*She stopped. What was it?*

*"Fantastic," he supplied. "I think I stopped*
*breathing there for a full minute. Jesus."*

*In truth, she might have said it was very good.*
*Damn good, actually. She was languid in the water*
*in his arms, content, her heart slowing to a more*
*reasonable pace.*

*It was unfortunate they were enemies, locked in*
*a struggle he didn't even recognize.*

*That was fine; she preferred to be in control.*

*But still, too bad. They might have been great*
*together.*

# ONE

I t wasn't like the dress was really over the top.

Might just be the body in it.

Nick Fattelli took a sip from his snifter and negligently set it aside, watching, but he wasn't the only one. He was pretty sure every man in the room had turned to look.

The woman who had just come into the room was not even classically beautiful. Long dark hair, yes, he approved of that, and the sultry unusual eyes to set it off. Her skin was flawless, but her features were not perfect. That was fine—he wasn't looking for perfect. A tilt to the eyes, just a hint, and a shade of a Roman nose, but still she was very striking. The dress didn't hurt either, cut low enough to showcase her firm breasts and tight enough to accentuate what he thought was a world-class ass.

He approved 100 percent.

"Reign."

He turned and glanced at the man who had apparently caught him staring. "What?"

"That's her first name. Reign." Joey Carre took a small round cracker topped with pink shrimp and herb-flecked cheese from a tray and somehow managed to pop it into his mouth and still make the movement look sophisticated. He chewed and swallowed before he commented, "Saw you looking. Long stare, about two seconds over the ordinary. Don't worry, you aren't the first."

Of that, he had no doubt now that he'd seen her. "Okay, guilty as charged. . . . The story?"

Carre knew everyone. Maybe it was his connection with the fashion icons in a city where how a person was dressed told you more about them than a background check. Carre was slightly overweight, but the cut of his jacket fooled the eye, and his fair hair was thinning just enough to accent a high forehead and austere features. His eyes were a very pale blue and, rumor had it, missed nothing.

"She's connected."

Nick believed that. Their circles were fairly tight, this party an example. He glanced around the penthouse, saw the sleek furnishings and the tall shining windows that gave way to a terrace overlooking New York City. The skyline was brilliant through the wall of windows, and the floor was polished marble. Ten million bucks, easy, for this place. . . . The invitations were not passed out on street corners. "To?"

"Practically everyone, but not what you are

thinking right now." Joey shook his head and took a sip of champagne. "She's a pretty face, but it doesn't stop there."

So . . . intelligent, gorgeous in her own way, and willing to walk into a party like this one wearing a flamboyant green dress with all that ebony hair spilling down her back. . . . Good presentation. Every other woman had on the classic little black number. She stood out.

He admired her style. "Fashion?" He acted like it was a guess. He knew where her studio was and had even done a background check on her assistant.

"*And* good taste. They don't always go hand in hand." Carre looked affable, but Nick actually rarely thought that was his true persona. Carre added succinctly, "She's good. Just starting really to break in."

"Married?" He asked it politely enough, though he already knew the answer. Several offers in her past, but the one "yes" hadn't worked out.

He knew pretty much everything about her; they just hadn't met yet.

"Married? Absolutely not." Carre looked non-committal. "Not in the market either."

Good both ways. So was Nick.

He shot his cuffs. "Introduce me."

"You don't want to play with this one."

Nick's smile was ironic. "I think I get to make that decision on my own, don't you agree? Since you know her, let me rephrase. Please introduce me."

Carre shrugged and shook his head, those pale blue eyes appraising. "Fine. But I'm telling you, she's not looking. Robert Philliponi has been trying for months. She barely gives him the time of day."

"I admire her taste already."

He didn't care for the man. Philliponi's name had been linked to several hits, and he was under surveillance. Nick kept his distance as much as possible out of a finely honed sense of self-preservation. No harm in being at the same party like this one, because there were a lot of influential people, from socialites to politicians, but he would never want to hang one-on-one. Bad idea. He didn't need the association.

Nick followed Carre through the crowd, stopping now and then to greet someone, the room humming with music and dozens of conversations, before they finally reached the corner where his quarry stood talking to an elderly man and another woman. The woman was far too young to be the older man's wife but had her hand possessively on his well-tailored sleeve. Nick didn't recognize either one of them.

"Rupert Hanover," Carre murmured. "You might want to meet him. Owns several trucking companies, which isn't the most glamorous way to make over fifty million dollars a year, but obviously the blonde is willing to overlook it."

"Wife?"

"Not yet but give her time. Did you know she used to be married to a state senator?"

"I didn't know she existed," Nick said truthfully. And he still didn't, really, his gaze fastened on the dark-haired woman in the green dress. She turned when she caught sight of them approaching, and she smiled, presumably for Carre, since she didn't know Nick.

Yet.

Gorgeous green eyes framed by long lashes flashed a glance at him, and then took a long second look.

He looked right back.

"Hurry up and introduce me," he said under his breath, the evening taking on an intriguing promise.

Even though she'd worn the fuck-me dress, Reign really wasn't in the mood for a party.

Yes, the glitter of the skyline was gorgeous, the food was no doubt delicious—though she wasn't all that hungry after her frustrating day—the expensive clothing of the crowd both flamboyant and outrageous, or else extremely tailored, depending on the individual, and usually she liked the sophisticated hum of a gathering like this. . . . But not tonight.

Therefore, she had very little patience for the over-effusive—yet unmistakably hostile, she was getting the vibe loud and clear—woman stuck to Mr. Hanover. Reign wanted to just say out loud, *Don't worry about it, sweetheart, he's all yours,* but that would be a little blunt even for her, and she'd learned a long time ago that speaking her mind wasn't always the best idea.

So when she saw Joey Carre approaching, she was infinitely grateful. It wasn't like they actually worked together, but they crossed paths often in their business and he was pretty much someone she might consider a friend. "Pretty much" meant that she trusted not that many people, and she didn't trust him exactly, either, but whether it was naive or not—she didn't *distrust* him.

Crazy, but then life was pretty crazy most of the time.

The tall man with him was not familiar, and she would have remembered him if she'd seen him before.

*For sure.*

Nice face. Angular but still handsome enough. Good body, if a girl liked them long and lean and athletic looking. Dark hair, and to her surprise, blue eyes—hardly a pale Scandinavian blue, but a dramatic Mediterranean blue that set off his Italian coloring.

She did her best to not stare.

Great suit. It was her job, after all, so she always had an eye for style. Hand-tailored to his broad shoulders and perfectly fitted. She wouldn't have picked that tie, but she learned something new every single day; it worked, actually. A midnight hue to match the unusual color of his eyes, the pattern almost so low-key she didn't notice, but when he approached, she saw it was a shadowy block down the length of the expensive silk. The play of dark color against his white shirt was stylish and made a statement quite different from the vibrancy of her dress.

An opinion of him immediately started to form. She normally liked to be noticed; he didn't want to be noticed at all.

That was interesting.

It could be that he was pretty noticeable in the first place. Not just his height and those nice wide shoulders, but he had some pretty delicious hair going on—dark and wavy, cut expertly someplace expensive—his jaw slightly square but not too much, his arched brows over those cobalt eyes, and his slightly diffident air didn't reflect what she thought was a dangerous edge underneath.

She *knew* dangerous men. Her whole life they'd been there. Godfathers, uncles, cousins . . . her sixth sense was geared toward feeling the difference between people who made the rules and those that broke them. It didn't mean they were bad guys. . . . It wasn't that cut and dried. It was more how it was all handled. There were rules, and there were *rules*. Not everyone viewed them the same way, and for that matter, not everyone had the same rules in the first place.

This man was, hands down, a rule-breaker.

The worst sort of man for her.

But *fuck,* she liked his smile. It was a really boyish mesmerizing curve of his lips, though cute would never apply to his sophisticated image. Maybe it would be better described as deliberate, and as a rule she was absolutely not susceptible to that. She could seduce, but she couldn't *be* seduced.

At least before this moment.

"I'm Nick," he said in a low, smooth whiskey voice. Just a hint of some place other than New York in there. Italy maybe. It was hard to place.

"Reign. Think royalty and not weather." She took his fingers and judged the tensile strength there. No attempt to convince her he was a man by crushing hers—thank God—but enough pressure to let her know he was interested. She'd already gathered that, yet it was good to know he could play on the nice side of the team.

Unless he needed to play it rough. She hated herself a little for the flicker of interest. All her life, it had been this delicate balance between the good guys and the bad ones, but that wasn't so easy, she was discovering.

Some men were mostly bad. She'd met them, shunned them, and ran the other way as fast as she could whenever possible. Some thought they were good—she almost hated those self-righteous bastards even more—but she was in her thirties now, and one truth just kept popping up.

No one was all good, and no one was all bad. That was unfortunate. It would make it so much easier to make wise choices.

Around them the room worked, the people moving, the conversations humming, the music playing—something low, Puccini's "O Mio Babbino Caro," she thought—and a waiter passed with a plate of stuffed mushrooms, but they both shook their heads.

"Interesting first name," he said.

"My parents were a little eccentric as a couple."

He let go of her hand with a deliberate reluctance. "Can you tell me that story over a drink?"

Joey had already left, maneuvering away from them, taking the future Mrs. Hanover and her prey with him. No one could work a room like Joe. It wasn't like Reign and the new arrival were alone, but apparently he'd read the signs and decided to give them some space.

She read the signs too.

Mr. Fattelli had *asked* for an introduction. Reign weighed her response, and the pause was long enough for him to acknowledge it. Good. She wanted him to know she didn't talk to every guy that hit on her. The gleam of amusement in his eyes settled the deal. She said, "Johnnie Walker Black. Rocks, please."

"I like the lady's choice. Be right back."

She watched him go to the bar, saw him flash that killer smile at the female bartender who definitely returned it, and then he was shouldering his way back through the crowd, drinks in hand. He drank bourbon neat, she noted, two fingers in his glass.

"Thank you." Their fingers brushed as she accepted the drink, and she caught his gaze for a moment.

"Terrace?" he suggested. "It's a little difficult to carry on a conversation in here."

She took a sip and nodded. People were watching

them already, but she didn't care too much as he moved back politely to let her walk in front of him through the open glass doors.

A gentleman. That scored him a point.

They were hardly alone there either, but then again, it was a warm clear night. Still, it was a lot more intimate than the jammed apartment. Mostly there were couples, standing around talking.

"Reign?" he prompted, his eyes inquiring. "Your name? You promised me the story."

She lifted her shoulders. *Why not tell him?* "My mother's idea. I think the basic concept was that every single day I should be reminded that I am in charge of my own life. Not to let anyone tell me what to do and when to do it. Reign Supreme. Supreme. Can you believe that is my given middle name?"

"I admit that's a new one to me. Do you live up to it?" His hand moved his glass casually to his mouth, and he took a small drink, watching her.

*Hell yes, I do.*

"I think Joey will confirm I do. Tell me, Mr. Fattelli, what do you do?"

"I'm an investment banker."

"Just that?"

"Mostly."

A little oblique. Well, maybe he was into finance, but she knew that wasn't all he was from the dangerous glitter in his eyes.

If he was too evasive, she'd be smart to walk away. Her career was going well, and though not having an active romance wasn't perfect in her estimation, it wasn't bad either. She loved her job and people left her alone. She moved in the inner circles but did not actually have to be part of them.

All of it under control. Well, most of the time. The lure of the Life existed. It was practically all she knew. It stood in front of her at the moment in the guise of a handsome man with those striking eyes. . . . He represented danger, and she had the golden ticket for that ride.

She knew at that moment she was going to go home with him and give him the fuck of the century.

Bad boys were a weakness of hers, and she had the feeling he was a very bad boy indeed. Before he could answer the question, she said abruptly, "No. Don't tell me. I don't want to know after all. Is there any chance you want to give me a ride home?"

# TWO

She didn't live in Manhattan, but on Staten Island, so the drive was not exactly short.

He didn't really care.

Nick was interested in the lady, not her house. Those remarkable emerald eyes, for one, drew him in. She seemed to have almost a feline capacity to study him in a way that didn't let him know in the least what she was thinking.

*Rule one: always be able to read the mind of your opponent.*

He couldn't quite read her.

"What?" Reign asked when they crossed the bridge, her voice holding a hint of amusement. She crossed her elegant legs and he heard the whisper of silk. If he was a betting man, he'd swear she wore stockings and garters just to tantalize every man who came within her sphere . . . but maybe no panties?

That was sexy alone. A mini-fantasy. If she did wear them, he thought while trying to look casual, they would be something slinky and black, but her ass was memorable in that tight-fitting dress without a hint of a line. . . .

Black thong to match all that long, shining hair? Call it a personal weakness, but he did like long hair and hers was sleek and pure ebony. He wanted to touch it, but there was a much bigger problem at hand.

Who the fuck wanted her dead and *why*?

"I was thinking about your underwear." He said it candidly and with a slight grin. "Sorry. Guy thing."

Streetlights flashed by, and he wondered if he might not get a smack in the face for being so honest, but after a moment she burst out laughing. "You were sitting there with that look on your face because you were curious about my lingerie?"

"I never said I was deep." He raised his brows and expertly passed a city bus that was about to pull out. Driving these streets meant you needed to pay attention.

She sobered. "That is a lie. Don't try and fool someone who has trotted around this planet a time or two. You are extremely deep, Nicky." Her brows rose. "Do you mind if I call you that? We are, after all, discussing my underwear. The familiarity shouldn't bother you."

He could give back smartass. "As of this moment, I know nothing about your underwear, so I am not sure we should be giving each other nicknames."

Damn her, he was getting a hard-on. It wasn't that he didn't like women—he loved women—but he knew she was doing it deliberately and he never fell for that crap.

Maybe until now.

Her calf was perfection. Completely female in the curve, and his gaze followed it up to where her skirt met her knee. He really needed to pay attention to his driving.

She hiked up her skirt just a notch above those smooth thighs right at that moment. Still no underwear in sight—unfortunately not *that* high—but he was getting the idea. Reign said coolly, "I like how you look and move. You're going to have to take my word I don't do this with every man I meet, and maybe you don't care one way or the other, but when we get to our destination, I'd like to invite you in."

She slightly spread her legs and Nick sucked in a deep breath. Nothing unladylike in her movement, just crossing her legs on the other side, but the way she did it implied that "in" did not mean her apartment.

Oh, she was doing everything right. Playing him. He still couldn't see if she was wearing panties or not, and for now the fantasy eclipsed the reality anyway. Luckily, if he adjusted his jacket, she couldn't see how aroused he was, but then again, he was pretty sure she knew.

"I'd like to come in," he said, chagrined his voice held a slight hoarseness. That was embarrassing. He was known for being cold as ice.

This woman was trouble.

His entire working life he'd been warned he should watch for that *one*.

*The target that made you weak.* His father had explained it to him when he was in his teens in succinct terms. It wasn't like he hadn't already suspected maybe his parent didn't have a regular nine to five, but it was a little bit of a shock to know he was being groomed to take over the family business.

*You have two lives. Like everyone else, son. One in which you do the job, and one in which you have the other entity. Father, son, brother. It isn't any different than being a race car driver or the CEO of a company. . . . Those occupations aren't quite understood by people who don't do them, so just look at it with that attitude and you'll be fine.*

*But someday you might doubt yourself. You will find that one mark you can't hit because of emotional involvement. Just decline the job and walk away. What happens next is not your problem.*

But it was in a certain way. He was trying to make sense of this and not having any luck so far. She wasn't a logical target. It bothered him and he hated loose ends.

She murmured, "Good. We understand each other pretty well right away. I like that. Where are you from anyway? I've been trying to place your accent but can't quite put my finger on it."

"I'm of Italian descent."

"Believe it or not, I figured that out already." Her voice was dry. "And I've met men like you before. That translates directly to: I will never tell you who

I am exactly, so maybe you shouldn't ask too many questions."

"Smart girl."

"Woman. I promise you I haven't been a girl for a very long time, Nicky."

His gaze dropped to her full breasts in a deliberate stare. "I stand corrected. Woman. Yep. Totally agree."

Softly she said, "I'll help you out with that in a few minutes."

"What?"

"Your hard-on."

"What makes you think . . ." It was a reflex to want to deny it, but he had just shifted on the seat again, and actually, it was true, so after a moment he just looked into those emerald eyes and murmured instead, "I'm really looking forward to it."

She reached out and deftly flicked his jacket open, pressing her hand between his legs as if measuring the length of his erection. "Uhm, nice."

It felt good. A little too good, and he liked her bold sense of self. Not flamboyant—that usually turned him off rather than on—but alluring because she was confident and sexy.

He removed her hand and lifted it to his lips, kissing her palm. "Why do I have the feeling this is going to be a very enjoyable evening?"

"How flattering. Smarter than you look."

"That is one hell of a backhanded compliment, Ms. Reign Supreme. How do I come across?"

"Dangerous. And you know it. Oh hell, be careful."

He narrowly missed a cab, hearing the blare of the horn. He probably did deserve the finger on that one.

Reign withdrew her hand and murmured, "That was close. Sorry."

"You are kind of a distracting passenger." An understatement.

"I doubt that you aren't aware of my family's business ventures."

Someday his heart rate would return to normal. "That makes me look stupid?"

"I never said that, did I? I think the implication was that involvement with me can be a risk, and at first impression you seem like a man who plans his every move."

Nick laughed, paying a lot more attention to his driving. "Why do I feel like we are talking in circles here?"

"Maybe a little. How often do you tell the truth, Mr. I'm-of-Italian-Descent?"

"Never," he said and touched her. Just a slight resting of his hand on her thigh, but when she didn't object, he slid his hand up under her skirt—hell, she'd done it essentially to him—and found the answer to his question.

No underwear.

And she was wet. He slipped two fingers inside her easily, and she made a small very sexy sound.

How perfect. He was hard as hell and she was ready for it.

He drove a Bentley, wore tailored clothing, but Reign was fairly street-smart and knew that her first impression was absolutely correct. Pure bad boy, through and through.

Why the hell that made the game more exciting she'd have to examine later, but introspection, she'd learned over the course of what so far was a colorful life, was not necessarily a good tactic.

*So,* she said to herself, *don't think about this too much*.

He'd be good in bed. She knew it. He did something interesting with his thumb that made her inner muscles tighten in response while he still managed to drive with skillful attention after their near miss.

Finesse. Not all men had it. Reign had never been interested in selfish lovers. Lifelong commitment? Not necessary. It wasn't that she didn't desire that someday. . . . But she'd been betrayed once—badly—and as a result, she'd acquired some very good defensive skills and a more worldly view of life.

"That's nice." She moved a little against his hand. "Hopefully, it's a promise of a memorable evening."

"I'll take good care of you." He looked into her eyes as he slid his hand out from between her legs.

Oh, he better. Trust was earned, not just given freely.

It was the rule by which she lived her life.

She had no desire to get burned and the resolve to make sure it didn't happen.

Reign moved her skirt down a few inches. "I was hoping you might. Words are just words though. Deliver."

Nick smiled, gorgeous in his expensive suit, his posture relaxed. "I intend to."

Then he licked his fingers.

Slowly. Like he savored the intimate taste of her. And maybe he did, for he started to set his hand on her knee again, and Reign stopped him. "I'm pretty sure you can do that better in my bedroom, and we're almost there."

"I hope it's damned close."

"Are we in a hurry?"

"I am."

"Then you're in luck." She pointed. "This is it. Park in the drive if you want."

"Here? A house?"

Yes, a house. Not a ritzy apartment in a high-rise building downtown with a gym, rooftop deck, and doorman. She owned a house because her son deserved the best upbringing possible. She liked it too. Two stories and brick, with great landscaping—not that she had the time, she paid someone to do that—but it was perfect for her right now. Maybe, when Vince left for college, she'd choose something else, but for now . . . home.

Vince was away with friends who owned a vacation home on Long Island, and she was getting a taste of that freedom. She adored her only child, but this break might just be what nudged her to invite a sexy stranger home for the first time in . . . she couldn't remember.

"I like the quiet."

Nick parked, slid out of the driver's seat, and went around to open her door. "Fine with me." He took her arm as they went up the steps to the front door. "Nice place."

She could tell him that her father had loaned her the money for the down payment, and she'd worked two jobs to make it happen because she'd paid every single dime back, but she tended to be a private person when it came to financial information.

To any personal information, really. And all she knew about him was that he had a damned sexy smile.

"Thanks." She unlocked the front door and went to press a button to disarm the alarm system, but the light wasn't blinking and she didn't hear the beep to signal she should turn it off. Maybe she'd forgotten to turn it on; she'd been in kind of a hurry when she'd left. "That's strange. The alarm system is disarmed."

"Ever happen before?" Nick's voice was casual but his stance suddenly wasn't. Like a light flicking on.

"Not that I can recall but I admit I might have forgotten. I was late for the party." She really had been. "Care for a drink?"

He looked around the foyer and she didn't mistake that sweeping appraisal. *Rule two: available exits accounted for*. Nick said pleasantly, "If you're having one, I will too, but don't go to any trouble."

Reign dropped her keys in a bowl on a polished marquetry table. "I might. Or I might not want to wait."

"However you want to play it."

Good answer. She liked having control. Stepping out of her heels, one by one, she deliberately gave him a nice view of her ass as she bent over to set her shoes aside. "That's better."

"That's perfect," he said with proper appreciation, one shoulder braced against the wall. "You know, I think I'm more hungry than thirsty."

"We could order a pizza." Her tone was facetious because she knew exactly what he meant.

"Yeah, well, I was thinking of something a little different." He straightened, and she had to admire the smoothness of the lithe masculine movement.

"As in?"

"I've had a taste of you. I liked it." He reached for her, but did it slowly enough she didn't take a reflexive step back. "Can we explore the possibilities?" Nick's hands settled on her shoulders. "I like exploring." His mouth on her neck was warm and teasing. "Care to guide me to the closest bed?"

"I'll show you."

"Just tell me." In a bold theatrical move he simply picked her up and inclined his head toward the stairs. "That way?"

*Put me down.*

She almost said it, but then again, she'd been the one to suggest he come home with her, and if she was anything, she was honest. "Top of the stairs, but I can walk."

"I can carry you." He started up.

"Cut the caveman stuff. No point has to be proved here."

"Is that what I'm doing?"

"I'm not sure."

"Are we already arguing?"

She had to laugh because his grin was very engaging. And really, he had the most incredible eyes. The carrying-her-up-the-stairs was kind of a romantic touch, but she wasn't sure she wanted romantic. Hot, sweaty, and wild, absolutely.

Romance was optional.

"We're both Italian. Of course we are arguing. What did you expect?" Her arms circled his neck for balance. It was better if he was intent on doing this that they didn't fall down. That would definitely spoil the mood.

"You have a point."

"First door on the left."

The door to her bedroom was almost shut.

Open only one telling inch.

*What?*

Reign's body froze. Her son wasn't home, and she sure as hell knew she had left that door wide open, and the alarm had been off, which wasn't telling if each incident was singular, but together it really bothered her. "Put me down."

At that moment she was glad Nick was everything she suspected he might be, because he dropped her on her feet and drew a weapon from behind his back with what looked like fairly impressive precision. The gun fit his hand naturally and he was comfortable with it. That didn't surprise her at all somehow.

"We got a problem here?" he asked her, slanting a razor-sharp glance her way, but she knew his attention was on that almost-shut door.

Reign said a prayer of thanks that Vince was far away and nodded. "I think so."

# THREE

Nick didn't kick the door open. That was for the inexperienced.

They stood in a long dark hallway, a series of doors to his right, nothing to the left except an oak railing to protect against the drop down into the foyer. It looked nice, but there wasn't really anywhere to escape.

"Talk to me," he said quietly. "Who do you think is in your bedroom and what do you believe they want from you?"

Reign rebelled at first. "You don't have to fight my battles."

He wasn't surprised, but this wasn't the time to get independent. He was armed, but in that clingy dress, there was no doubt *she* wasn't concealing a weapon. As pleasantly as possible, he urged, "Sweetheart, I'm not thinking it is a battle, but maybe a small war. So spill. Police? Or is this a private conversation?"

Those glorious green eyes were wide. "I honestly don't know. I can't see why it would be either one."

*Shit*. He believed her. Besides, police had no finesse. They didn't need it.

Private war, then. He said curtly, "Stay right here and I mean it."

She nodded, her glossy hair moving over her supple shoulders.

Why couldn't anything be simple?

*Connected*, Joey had told him. No doubt about it. Her entire family was in organized crime, but she really wasn't as far as he could tell. Her portfolio read up-and-coming fashion designer. True, her father and several uncles were doing time, so maybe this was related to making some kind of point to her relatives.

Okay. He understood that, but he didn't like it was her house, that she was alone—or might have been—because while there was no particular honor system for getting even, killing wives or daughters or children was not part of how it all worked. Nick stepped back and eased open the door. He usually just carried a Glock .45. Light, easy to fire, and effective. That was why law enforcement liked them, and he didn't disagree. He entered with the weapon extended in his hands and immediately, like a dog catching a scent, registered a waft of aftershave.

*Checkmark*. Some operatives were so fucking careless.

He liked her bedroom. Sleek, like her, with a sleigh bed on a polished dark wood floor, and a bedspread in shades of white and black. A huge armoire in the corner. One lamp in the corner on a lacquer table, and some large framed prints on the walls, all in black and white to match the bedspread. A patterned rug. He thought she'd probably designed it herself, since it looked really nice and word was she was good at what she did.

*Where are you?*

Closet? Probably. The room was proportioned big enough to handle the size of the bed and an en suite bathroom—he took a swift glance inside and it seemed to be empty—so the closet was a logical choice.

Someone was there, or had been there if she was right about the door, and he thought Reign was pretty tuned to the essentials of self-preservation.

"Come on out," he ordered. "I'm not all that interested in you living through the night, but the lady doesn't want blood on her floor."

The bullet grazed his shoulder. Nick swung to the side, weapon extended, and fired four rounds into the door. Her closet would never be the same, he thought philosophically as he crouched down by the bed, but Reign was still alive, and surely that was what mattered.

What most people didn't realize was that guns were really loud, especially if fired in small spaces. He couldn't hear anything except for the ringing in his ears in the aftermath. That was why he didn't know Reign had run into the room.

No return fire.

When she grabbed his arm, he said, "Jesus, get back. I don't know if he's dead. I thought I told you to stay in the hall."

"Look." She pointed, and he realized there was a spreading pool of blood coming out from under the door, but he had no idea how many of them there might be.

"If I got one, that doesn't mean it was all of them." He pushed her back behind him. He was at least twice the size of her, so as a shield, he would work pretty well.

And this was, after all, his forte.

Actually, he was better at elimination than protection, but he was always up for a new challenge.

For now his concern was whoever might be bleeding out in her closet, since he hadn't heard a sound from them yet.

It meant nothing. If Nick was trapped with a bullet in him, he'd play dead too.

Nick approached slowly and slanted his body against the wall, gun extended in one hand.

No noise.

His entire life he'd known it was possible he might walk into a bullet. A given. Since he was old enough to start to realize the Life was part of his legacy, he'd gotten it. Maybe it was in his blood.

*Fuck it.*

He reached over and opened the door, taking his chances.

Quite the romantic evening.

Reign began to reassess. So . . . she'd brought a stranger home, there had been someone who wanted to kill her in her bedroom, said stranger had shot him through the door, and it was just another night in the suburbs.

Not quite.

Try explaining *that* to the cops.

"I met Mr. Fattelli at a party and invited him over for a drink," she said again, still polite, but she was starting to get a bit strained.

The officers had been nice enough, especially since her alarm had been clearly tampered with, but she was getting tired of telling the same story over and over. As far as she could tell, a man had been hiding in her bedroom. That was not *her* fault.

It did shake her up, and that didn't help when it came to answering the barrage of questions.

The lead detective was a thin older man with gray hair and the darkest eyes she'd ever seen, and she'd met a lot of Italians in her life. His name was Candelaria and he smiled diffidently, but she wasn't fooled. They were sitting in her living room, done in taupe and bronze, with the antique Italian chandelier she'd ordered from Tuscany when she decided to splurge. It was gorgeous with original sconces, and though she had to stand on a chair to light it, it was worth it for ambiance.

Tonight was not the night, however. Not as they carried out a dead body.

"I've said I didn't see it happen. More than once."

"I'm sorry, Ms. Grazi, but when it comes to a possible homicide, you are going to always have to say it more than once."

Candelaria looked patient—but he wasn't. She

knew men fairly well, and he was doing his best, but he wasn't into her hesitation, and that wasn't doing her any favors.

She leaned forward, looked into the man's eyes, and spoke very plainly. "Detective. I was in the hallway when it happened. But I will tell you this—again—Nick Fattelli walked into my bedroom on the assumption there was an intruder, and he was right. We all know the intruder shot first, I heard it, and that first shot was completely different from the others. If Nick killed him, I'm not experiencing a lot of regret because that man shot first."

"You just met and he risked his life for you?" He did look skeptical.

"Don't you do that every single day? Not for me specifically, but for people you don't know?"

"He is not a police officer."

"No." That was undeniably true. "He told me he's an investment banker and considering where we met this evening, I believe it. I'm sure you saw his car parked outside. I assume he has a legal permit for the gun he carries."

Those dark eyes looked right through her. "I am not talking to him, I am talking to *you*. So let me make sure we both agree on your statement. You picked up a man at a party, he came home with you, it was clear there was an intruder, someone was in fact in your closet and shot at him first, and Mr. Fattelli nailed him dead solid through the door."

Dead solid.

Her entire life she'd seen interesting events that made her wonder exactly about her placement on this earth. Oh sure, everyone had their own story, but hers surely qualified as being unique.

Fashion designer. Mob wife. Progeny of an infamous family.

Well, ex–mob wife, but it didn't help that her father was doing time for racketeering. . . . The circle always came around back to it.

"You think this had something to do with my . . . connections." It wasn't really a question.

He set aside his notebook and sighed. "I would be stupid if it didn't occur to me. Ms. Grazi, who do you think wants you dead?"

She glanced around Nick's apartment. "Nice place."

Nick—was that his real name? What the hell was she doing trusting him? Well, he *had* probably saved her life—smiled. "No dead guy in my closet. Gives it a special little extra something, don't you agree?"

"Maybe." She tossed her purse on the table and essayed a confident smile right back. "I'm a fool for coming here." Reign shook her long hair back over her shoulder. "I know it and you know it. I did text my sister to give her the address."

"Good idea. Always take precautions." He moved across the room toward a wine cabinet. Pale walls, bold paintings, and leather furniture. He had good taste. He splashed whisky into a crystal glass and came over to hand it to her. But his expression was amused and she felt naive. "This has been a somewhat eventful evening and maybe we should just sit and have a drink. That's all I have in mind."

"You want to just sit?" She sank into a gray chair that was sleek and modern, and then she provocatively crossed her legs.

"I just killed a man in your house." He took an opposite chair. "We were lucky on two counts. My prints were not anywhere, but nothing was wiped clean and they smelled organized crime all over it. The locals are pretty smart. The only reason we walked out of there."

"My father is—"

"You don't have to tell me." He settled down in a relaxed movement, his smile negating the interruption. "Come on, Reign, you know I know who you are. A Grazi."

"Then what the hell do you want?"

"Just one night. You were offering it before."

She had been. "Still am."

"Want a confession?"

"As long as I won't have to lie in court."

Nick started to laugh and it made him look infinitely lighter, maybe even boyish, which was hard for someone so masculine. He shook his dark head. "Not that kind of confession."

"Let's see, in one evening alone you've tasted my pussy—in a kind of secondhand fashion, by the way, and we need to fix that—and killed a man in my bedroom. I can't see what you could possibly say that would shock me."

"You have no problem saying 'pussy,' huh?" His expression was amused.

"None. I thought you knew who I was."

"Now you're just testing me."

She drained her drink. "If you are going to stick around, sweetheart, get used to that."

But the truth was, she was tired. Hours of talking to the police and the sense of violation from having her home a crime scene had killed any kind of romantic mood, and the only reason she hadn't insisted he take her to her sister's house was that she didn't want to go over it all again with Maria.

Maybe she had the right instincts, because then he said in an even voice, "What I want can wait. I have a guest bedroom. You look wiped out."

Salvatore listened carefully to the dialogue, discounted the part he knew was bullshit, and then reassessed the situation.

After all, he was his father's son.

Almost midnight. A hint of old smoke in the air, the clink of glasses, the sound of conversations, and the occasional burst of laughter. Typical bar atmosphere, with not quite enough illumination, the walls lined with old pictures, the scratched surface of the bar probably exactly the same as when his father first walked through the door quite a few years ago. Sal had his first drink in the place when he certainly wasn't legal and still stopped in now and again.

But he'd heard Reign's name, and it had hit him like a hammer. It wasn't like the name was common, and he was in a definite position to possess information he didn't even want to have, but there it was.

"So, correct me if I'm wrong, but the buzz is someone was killed in Reign Grazi's house tonight?"

The bartender eyed his plain T-shirt dubiously. "You just don't look like a wise guy."

The guy was new but at least wary. Always a good sign.

"I'm a college student and we're all broke," Sal said crisply, "so give me a break." He leaned his elbows on the bar.

No lie there. He was wrapping up a law degree.

"You do look kind of young."

Was twenty-eight young? He wasn't sure. "Yeah, well, in life experiences, I'm old as hell. Tell me about what happened?"

"How do I know you're not a cop?"

"How the hell do any of us know anything about each other? Do I seem like a cop? Besides, I take it the cops know already. My last name is Ariano."

The man put his beefy forearms on the counter and took a good long minute to consider it. "No," he said finally after an assessing look, "you don't seem like a cop, but you're right, who knows? You want information I'm not really all that anxious to give. I've had undercover in here before. Usually, they're pretty good at looking like they belong. But Ariano rings a bell."

Now they were getting somewhere.

"Who was he? The shooter who got killed, I mean. One of your regulars?"

"Did I say that?"

"Why the hell was he in her house?" Salvatore looked around. The place had pool tables and vinyl-covered bar stools, and even more cigarette smoke was in the air now. Not at all the style of the woman he knew. Reign was more inclined to stop into a classy Manhattan establishment. "*She* doesn't come in here, does she?"

"A lot of people come in here."

"I take it one of them is the man who was shot. What was his name? They'll release it in the papers, so why not just tell me?"

In response he got a stony look and the comment, "If you think he was here legally, you are dead wrong. That's about all I have to say."

This was getting him nowhere, but he shouldn't be all that surprised. The bar was owned by one of his father's friends, and he knew that it was patronized almost exclusively by people who had ties to organized crime, and that, of course, included himself.

The basis of his relationship with Reign wasn't just the mutual attraction, but that they had a lot of mutual history.

Tossing a few bills on the counter, he went outside and called her cell. It rang but she didn't answer. Considering the hour and the evening she'd probably had, he wasn't all that surprised.

So he decided to call Vince.

The kid liked late hours so Sal wasn't worried. Once Salvatore had called him a vampire and the kid just laughed and said, "Hey, man, it's quiet.

That's the perfect time to play video games or read a book, or whatever. I'm not a geek but kind of into quiet."

No, Reign's son was not at all a geek, but he was pretty bright, and if she was really worried, Vince would know. "Hi V. What are you doing?"

"Hanging out on Long Island. I haven't heard from you in a while, Sal. What's up?"

He sounded fine. Not upset . . . not anything but like a normal teenager. Sal didn't have enough facts to get the kid all worried. No use in that, because it was Reign's place to tell her son about the shooting and she obviously hadn't yet. He just wanted more information, and this was apparently not the source. Easily, he said, "Nothing really. Just thinking of you and knew you were a night owl. Hey, didn't realize you were out of town with friends."

Educated guess. Reign had done a good job with him and was up and coming with her career, but she did not have a house on Long Island, or at least not one that he knew of, and he was fairly sure he knew everything about her.

Because he loved her. Not like a little, but the real deal, full devotion and all the crap that came along with it, which at this moment meant that he was worried sick but didn't want to dump Vince into the same hole.

"We left a couple of days ago." There was a shrug he couldn't see but sensed in Vince's tone. He was Reign all over again: green eyes, that jet-black hair, and those amazing cheekbones. "I'm having a good enough time."

And he was out of harm's way.

*Because there was a dead man in your mother's bedroom earlier....*

No one was shot in another person's closet unless there was something bad going down.

Salvatore said with what he hoped was equanimity, "Tell your mom when you talk to her I said hi."

Vince sounded a little puzzled over the purpose of the call, but he said, "Sure. She called earlier too.... Is there a reason?"

"Nope."

"Okay then, gotta go. We're going to go swimming. Full moon tonight."

"Have fun." Salvatore hung up the phone and sat there, rubbing his temple. He wanted to try Reign again, but he had sworn he wouldn't after their last conversation. Never should he have told her he loved her. He was a smart guy, he knew better, but it had just slipped out in the aftermath of making love to her in the pool they'd shared that last night, the warm feel of her in his arms so comfortable he'd almost made an even worse mistake and asked her to marry him.

More than once she'd said firmly she would never ever get married again. It was off the table.

*Especially to someone from* his *family* was the unspoken ending to that declaration. His father and her father hated each other, and in a different world, that might be not speaking to each other at the country club, but in the Life, there could be unpleasant consequences to a feud that ran as deep as theirs.

Sal should never have slept with her in the first

place. Reign sure as hell shouldn't have slept with him. It probably would never have happened if either of them had given their last names when they met.

He stared at his phone and even pulled up his contact list. "Fuck," he muttered and resisted the urge to press that button and try her cell again.

# FOUR

He'd left her alone the night before.

Nick watched her sleep—he didn't sleep much himself. A few hours and he was good to go, but Reign hadn't had the easiest evening. He'd admired the way she'd handled it all, but near the end he'd known she was simply too tired to do anything else but strip off her clothes and fall into bed.

He really, really approved of the stripping part. She might be in his bed—she'd not opted for the guest room and he thought that maybe, just maybe, the reason why was that as strong as she might be, she didn't want to be alone—but he hadn't touched her because she'd fallen asleep almost immediately and hadn't given him permission.

His mother had raised him to be a gentleman. Pure Sicilian, she tolerated no bad behavior from her sons, and he'd learned that the hard way a time or two because his father had backed her up every single time, and he was not a man to take lightly.

So Nick propped himself on one elbow and just . . . watched.

The gentle lift of her chest as she breathed. Very nice. Her breasts were full compared to her frame but looked real. Perfect pink nipples and firm flesh with a natural feminine shape. No enhancement there. She kept herself fit with smooth muscle tone to her arms, and she wasn't a sylph but still slender. Good, he was a pretty tall guy and didn't like women he felt he might break if things got a little interesting in bed.

Reign could hold her own. It was that sense of self he'd liked right from their first meeting.

Yes, he'd protected her, but he wasn't 100 percent sure she couldn't have handled the situation all by herself.

Long dark lashes fluttered as she started to wake up.

Great timing. He had a raging hard-on. They'd been cheated out of their first night, but maybe they could make up for it now.

Lightly, he ran his fingers down the length of her arm. "Hmm. Good morning, *bella*."

She rolled to her back, but didn't cover herself. "I can't believe I slept like that in a strange place."

He couldn't help but admire the view, and he had his reasons for not being very surprised over the shooting. He knew a lot more than she did.

It pleased him to realize she didn't often sleep

anywhere but her own house. "I think you might
have needed it."

"I think so too." She sat up and pushed her hair
back in a graceful movement, the sheet around her
waist, those spectacular breasts bared. No modesty,
but with tits like hers, what woman would care? On
a beach in Rio she'd make jaws drop. "What time
is it?"

"It's Sunday. Doesn't matter." Nick wanted to
touch her but wasn't sure how it would be received.
Gorgeous woman in his bed, one he didn't really
know, even though they'd been through an interesting experience together. . . . Life was full of new
twists and turns.

She yawned. "I'm a designer. I literally work seven
days a week because I basically work for myself."

"Considering the circumstances, I think you can
take the morning off."

Reign seemed to fully wake up, memory flood-
ing back from the look on her face. "Oh shit, yeah,
last night. I remember now. It still feels like a bad
dream."

"Easy, babe." Nick gently pushed her back down
and looked into her eyes. "Here's the recap. No
charges pressed; he wasn't carrying ID and had disarmed the security system, but at least I was there,
had a license for the weapon I used, and I have no
record. Bet you he couldn't say the same."

She caught his wrists. "He couldn't say *anything*.
You killed him. Investment banker? Bullshit. I know
a pro when I meet one."

To admit or deny? He'd already figured out she was smart, so a denial might just tick her off.

"I *am* an investment banker." He was, actually. And good at it.

"But that's not *all* you are."

True.

"So . . . I'm not an angel." He adjusted his position and nuzzled her neck. "But, let's face it, no one is. Are you going to hold that against me?"

"Does your arm hurt?"

"He just grazed me. Barely broke the skin." It was true. Just a scratch. It had barely even bled, and the medical examiner had actually bandaged it for him right at the scene. Nick had been a lot more unhappy about his damaged jacket. That suit was expensive. He murmured, "That isn't the part of my anatomy that's hurting right now."

"I can see that." She looked unabashedly at where his erection lifted the sheet. "At least let me brush my teeth."

"You're going to bite me? That sounds interesting." Nick smiled lazily and rolled to his back. At least that part of the conversation was out of the way. "Sure. Help yourself."

"I just might." She walked to the bathroom nude, unselfconscious, and he understood why. She had no need to be. Firm ass, all that dark hair . . . his cock was so hard it was painful. Before she went in the door, she turned. "You'd better have a condom."

He did. "No worries."

"Or two," she said just before she shut the door.

He groaned out loud, but he was at least grateful she couldn't hear it once the latch clicked.

There was no question that he liked confident women, but he'd also never met one that was quite so . . . different.

Yeah, that was how he'd describe her. *Different.* In his life, women had mostly all been the same. Obviously, like with anyone else, they took on certain roles, but Reign was a unique experience so far. She'd handled the night before well too: calm with the cops, obviously a little shaken up, but basically taking it all in stride. Their stories had meshed, and at the end of it all, there had been no reason law enforcement could find a probable cause to hold either of them—though he knew they'd tried because of her family name. And so here they were.

They'd hadn't known each other very long, but he hoped that was really what was about to change. Women liked him, but on some level, most of them were a little afraid of him. Reign didn't seem to be, or if she was, she was one hell of an actress.

She came out of the bathroom wet . . . literally.

Water beaded on her skin, those beautiful breasts slightly swaying, her dark hair damp. The triangle of dark hair between her thighs was trimmed but not entirely bare, which was just how he liked it. Reign flashed him a smile. "I had to take a quick shower. Hope you don't mind."

"Fuck no." Propped against the headboard, Nick inhaled through his nose and exhaled through his mouth in a controlled conscious effort. "At this moment, I'd swear I'd forgive you just about anything."

She took three leisurely steps across the rug he'd paid a fortune for, which was imported from some place he couldn't even identify as a country but felt like silk if you walked on it in bare feet. "You enjoy oral sex?"

"Both giving and receiving." That was one hell of an honest answer. If she put her mouth on him, he would last maybe a minute or two. . . .

He slid from the bed and caught her around the waist and tumbled her to her back on the silk sheets. "Let me go first. Spread your legs."

"I—"

"I have an agenda." He kissed the plane of her stomach. "You come, I come, and then we come together. . . . I'd really like to do it my way. You're going to like it."

"Don't try to control me."

His hands smoothed her hips. "Never. Say the word and I stop. Reign, you're safe with me."

She relaxed. He felt it happen. The tension left her muscles and she smiled genuinely for the first time since she'd met her. "Is that your line?"

"I don't have a line." Nick licked the tip of one very delectable breast. "Why would I bother with that?" His fingers explored the luxuriant abundance of her tits. They were firm and gloriously feminine. "I know I'm happy at the moment. These are . . . *very* nice."

"Yes, well, in my experience, every man has a line. I can't argue that part. You do feel happy." But she did sink her fingers into his hair, and from the arch of her back she seemed to really like it when he took her nipple into his mouth.

"I'm not every man." He murmured it against her warm skin. She tasted exotic, like vanilla and apricot, and he pressed his erection against her thigh.

Then he moved lower. And lower.

Pushed her thighs apart.

She bent her knees and opened wider, and when he parted her labia and tongued her clit, her lashes drifted down as she closed her eyes. A small inarticulate sound of enjoyment came from deep down in her throat.

Good. He really liked women who enjoyed sex and weren't afraid to show it, and he'd guessed that she would from the first moment he'd seen her walk into the party.

As he licked and gently sucked, her spine arched even more and she moaned, threading her fingers through his hair, taking over, giving him clear signals of when to back it off a little to delay her orgasm, prolonging the pleasure.

Smart girl. When he took two fingers and slid them inside her pussy, she was wet, hot, and tight, and it sent her over the edge. He finger-fucked her as she came. Nick kept her there until she twisted away and commanded, "Stop."

It was quite a sight, he decided as he rolled to his back, his erection pulsing with the beat of his heart, the veins visibly distending and subsiding. That luscious body sprawled on his bed flushed a tint of post-climax pink, her eyes only half-open as she caught her breath.

If his orgasm was half as good, he decided with an inner, purely male sense of satisfaction, this was going to be a really fantastic morning. The night he'd envisioned had been ruined, but it was a new day, new start, and quite frankly, he couldn't regret being there and what happened, because at least he'd been able to protect Reign, and in the unpleasant aftermath, no one except the unwanted intruder had been hurt.

Considering what that man had wanted him to do the last time they'd come face to face, it seemed like justice to him.

Not a bad start.

Reign had a feeling Nick was going to be a skillful lover, but also the sense that there was a bit of selfishness involved since he wanted her to return the favor.

No problem. Her last lover had wanted slow, romantic sex, whispered sweet things in her ear, and she was built more like a race car than a sedan meant for slow rides in the countryside. Fast and dirty was what sent her libido into high gear.

Fuck, he had *nice* muscular shoulders, not to mention a big cock. Brawny thighs and a flat stomach . . . in the morning light coming through the window, his body was gilded a light gold and he was beyond a doubt really ready to go. Even though his grin was a little cocky, she couldn't argue with it.

And she couldn't resist teasing him a little, even though he'd just been really, really nice to her.

Not to mention that he saved her life the night before. She didn't want to think about that too much, because not for a minute did she believe the man Nick had shot had been a burglar who heard their voices and ducked into her closet, which was how the police had treated it in the end.

For now, she was in bed with a very delicious Italian man who definitely knew his way around a woman's body, and she was going to worry about what happened a little later. Reign rolled over on her belly to give him a good view of her ass—she worked out to make sure it stayed nice and firm, more because *she* wanted to be comfortable with her body than to please anyone else—and lifted her brows. "You completed the first part of your 'agenda' pretty well. I get the impression it's my turn."

"You're not going to get an argument here."

"I take it you've been complimented on this before." She ran a finger up his impressive erection. The skin was satin smooth and hot. "I don't want you to get too conceited so I won't comment."

With her finger, she wiped off a bead of semen from the tip and licked it off. "Uhm. I changed my mind. I'll go ahead and say it. You have a really big dick."

"That's better than being *called* a really big dick. Your finger was nice but your tongue would be better." He reclined against the pillows and his voice had dropped to a husky timbre that betrayed he was pretty interested in what came next.

He should be. She gave one hell of a blow job. Sex was power, and power alone was sexy.

Slow and sultry, making him wait for it . . . Reign rose up on her knees and ran her hand over Nick's hard chest, looked him in the eyes, and smiled. "I suppose I owe you."

"It was my pleasure."

"I meant for being there last night."

"Forget last night. I thought you were referring to just a few minutes ago. You interested in paying me back?"

He really was a gorgeous man. The suit was nice, but now, naked and lounging on the bed, his hair tousled from sleep, his blue eyes slightly narrowed, he was . . . pretty delicious.

"Oh, you have no idea." She dropped her hand to his crotch and explored his balls, cupping his testicles.

He'd like it when she went down on him. Quite a lot.

Nick groaned as she fondled his sac.

She laughed and lowered her head, rolling the tip of her tongue around the head of his penis. The slight salty taste of his semen was like an aphrodisiac and she was wet and ready again. This was a test of sorts; he would admit that too, she suspected. The first crucial encounter did not just involve exploring each other's bodies but also a certain sense of communication that was unspoken but important.

That she'd fallen asleep in his bed after the events of the night before stunned her. Not just a little asleep, but dead asleep, and when she woke up she felt better than she had in a long time. There hadn't been a push for sex either, which she appreciated. It hadn't been the easiest of evenings, but quite frankly, bringing her to his place was better than having to get a hotel or go stay with people who would ask all kinds of questions. She'd been way too wiped out for that.

"Babe," he whispered as she took him in her mouth, his fingers tangling in her still damp hair and his breath coming out in a low hiss. "Sweet Jesus."

Sucking him deeper, she consciously relaxed the muscles in her throat, stroking his balls, and as predicted, he made an audible sound of enjoyment.

Circling his cock with her fingers, she began to pump it as she licked and sucked, and while he did last longer than most men, it still wasn't more than a minute or two before he said hoarsely, "Unless you swallow, maybe you'd better . . . oh shit . . . stop."

Once again a gentleman. At least he'd bothered to warn her.

She didn't let every man she slept with come in her mouth, but sometimes it felt good to be bad so she let it happen. Not to mention she really owed him, so when he came she milked it, part of it revenge for how he'd kept at her so she'd barely been able to breathe after consecutive orgasms, and part of it to prove a point.

*Meet Reign Supreme.*

When it was over he lifted her by her arms and rolled her to her back, pinning her down with his much larger body, their mouths inches apart. "If I can ever put two coherent thoughts together again, I'll be surprised." He nibbled on her neck, his dark hair like silk under her fingers. "Holy Mother of God, that was good. Give me about two minutes."

It took three, but that did include him slipping on the condom, and Reign noted his fingers were trembling at least a little, which sure hadn't happened when he killed the man in her bedroom. Then he'd been cold as ice.

He moved back over her, pressing her into the softness of the big bed, his knees nudging her legs apart. Those striking blue eyes held hers in a mesmerizing stare as he began to enter her. "I've eaten your pussy and you sure as hell have sucked me," he whispered. "I think it is time for a nice long slow fuck, right?"

She wrapped her legs around his waist. "I don't do anything slow."

His mouth curved in a smile as he penetrated deeper, inching in but taking care, considering his size. "Why is it I believe that?"

Already aroused, her body accepted his entry with pure female enthusiasm, so he slid in the rest of the way until he was fully embedded and Reign nipped at his lower lip. He really *was* big.

Then he kissed her. He hadn't before, which struck her as he slowly explored her mouth with his tongue, and a part of her wished he hadn't. Sex was sex, but kissing implied something else. Still, she liked the warm feel of his mouth against hers.

That was more dangerous than how fast he could pull a gun and put a bullet in someone he couldn't even see. Sex was fine. Kissing implied romance and she wasn't interested in romance, especially with someone in his profession, and she wasn't talking about investment banking. Besides, she'd known him less than a day.

"Are we waiting for some reason?" she whispered against his lips.

The worst part was that he got it. There was also some measure of surprise in his eyes that the kiss had even happened, and he slipped back into the persona of the man she'd met at the party, sophisticated and detached. The man who had killed someone the night before, after he'd taken a woman he'd just met home and never really blinked an eye.

"I never keep a lady waiting." Nick slid backward and then thrust into her willing body, the movement deliberate, his hands braced on either side of her shoulders as he filled her again in an erotic glide. "Remember my agenda? You came, and then I came, and now we need to do it together. You definitely took the edge off, sweetheart. I can last all morning."

It turned out he was a man of his word.

# FIVE

Reign took a bite of shrimp salad. "I was actually sore the next day."

"Seriously?" Giovanna leaned over the table.

With a shrug, Reign took a sip of wine. "Let's just say the phrase 'not all men are created equal' has meaning when it comes to Nick Fattelli."

"Introduce me?"

"Not on your life."

Her friend smiled mischievously, tossing back her hair, the bustle of the elegant restaurant in the background. They were at a table near the back, the glass windows showing the pedestrians passing on the street, everyone in a hurry, but then again, this was New York. Hurry was the order of the day. She leaned back in her chair. "Okay, now I *really* need to meet him."

Gio was a beauty with a voluptuous figure and

an engaging laugh. Nick would probably love her—
all men did, but at the moment Reign was not inclined to share. "Maybe down the line. Let's see
how it goes. Fair enough? If it doesn't work out,
you can have him."

"You like this one, huh?"

She wished it wasn't true. "I need a little time to
decide, that's all."

"Possessive? That's not you."

"Possessive for *now*." She took a sip of her iced
tea. "I'm playing this one day at a time. Vince is
always my top priority."

"He's registered and everything, right?"

"NYU and my family pulled no strings. He made
it on his own." She was really proud of him.

"Good for him." Giovanna glanced down at the
tabletop and then looked up. "The shooting . . .
everyone knows about it. You think they were after
Vince?"

"I don't know. He's his father's son." Reign blew
out a breath and stabbed a piece of avocado with
emphasis. "He has a grandfather and several uncles in prison. . . . If whoever set it up wanted to get
something from any of them, that would be the way
to do it. I'm telling you that would be a *mistake*.
My father would pull in every single debt he's owed,
so would his other grandfather. My son means
everything to both of them. It isn't wise to screw
round with either one of our families, much less
both."

"I don't disagree." Gio lifted a dark, perfectly
plucked brow. "I would go out on a limb and say it

isn't worth it to screw with *you* either. Word has it there was someone in your closet and he was actually shot through the door."

The network of information never failed to amaze her.

"He pointed a gun at the wrong guy," Reign confirmed. The avocado suddenly was tasteless. She set aside her fork.

"Apparently, since the shooter is dead."

"It bothers me." She only admitted it with a measure of reluctance. "Nick's very able to take care of himself. I'm not fooling myself there."

"Too able?" It was asked delicately, but Gio knew the Life.

"Probably. And they still haven't identified the intruder as far as I know. Maybe it's just really what they think. He broke in. We came home. The intruder panicked and found the first place to hide, then realized we were going to be in the bedroom for quite some time, and tried to scare us by taking a shot."

"That was his *big* mistake." Gio finished the last bite of her veal and dabbed at her mouth with her napkin. It was a gorgeous day outside, with sunny skies and the temperature already in the upper seventies. People passed their window, some talking and laughing, some frowning, at least half of them on their phones. "But, how did he get past the alarm?"

"The whole system was disabled. Otherwise I would have just slept in the spare room. Nick insisted I go home with him."

made up my mind not because of him, but for his own good."

"I don't think he'd agree."

"I lived through Ray's lies and cheating, my father's trial—my trust in men is shaky at best." Reign shook her head. "Sal needs someone with a less jaded outlook on life."

Gio stirred her tea. "The man who went to law school so he could represent his family in court? Yeah, don't sell him short. He's more of a realist than you give him credit for."

"I don't mean to sound superficial, but considering he's a good-looking guy, which he sure is, he doesn't need me because—can I point out again—he could have anyone."

"You know, Reign, and I'm just putting this out there, maybe you should let him decide. Yeah, he's a good-looking guy, and yes, he's in law school, and yes, there's all that stuff between your families, but you know, he's nice. And that hair . . . I've got to love the dark blond hair, but he still has that Italian nose."

Sal *was* actually blond, which wasn't as much of a surprise as some people might believe. His family was from the northern part of Italy, up near countries like Switzerland and Austria, and there was certainly some of that ethnic background in his blood. Flippantly, she responded, "You want to date him?"

"Hell yes." Giovanna sounded quite sincere but laughed to temper the moment. "I always have. But he doesn't seem interested, so we are just friends instead. I think we've known each other too long."

*Well, shit.*

Reign folded her arms. "Salvatore is off the table for me, so go for it. Mr. Fattelli is one of those men who can play the game. Sal doesn't play games at all."

"Life isn't a game, Reign. No one should know that more than you." Giovanna drained her glass and stood, her scarlet dress swirling around her calves. "I gotta run. Thanks for lunch."

Nick walked into the office at exactly four o'clock.

That was by his Rolex, and the thing had damn better keep accurate time.

"Have a seat." Carl Denton was thin, balding, of indeterminate middle age, and this particular afternoon he wore a suit that cost more than most people pay for their car.

"Mr. Denton." He took the indicated chair and settled in. "Thanks for seeing me."

"No problem, but I have a board meeting in fifteen minutes." Denton smiled like a shark, but that was appropriate; he was one.

"You know who I am?"

Denton said conversationally, "Yes, I do. Investment banking, correct?"

Very funny. Denton knew he was a man of varied skills. "I'd like some information."

"I don't ever—"

"Oh yes you do. Though we haven't met face to face, you once engaged my, shall we say, special talents. I always do my homework. Can we agree the job was done swiftly and discreetly and your messy little problem went away?" Nick kept his voice pleasant. For whatever reason, when he spoke in that reasonable tone, people got edgy. "I am sure everyone in the business knows I shot a man in Reign Grazi's bedroom a few nights ago, and I know it was a hired hit that didn't go as it was intended. My question is simple. We have a family thing going on here, or is this outside?"

"What makes you think I know?"

"I'm going to give you some advice." Nick smiled but he didn't mean it, and the man across from him understood that. "I'm pretty uninterested in playing games."

"Are you threatening me?"

"Oh God, no. If I was threatening you, you wouldn't have to ask." He raised his brows in inquiry. "So? The hit on Ms. Grazi?"

"Her father has a lot of friends in high circles. That usually means a lot of enemies."

"You in bed with him?"

"Her father?" Denton spread his hands. "We've some common business interests. It would be of no benefit to me to see his daughter out of the picture. As far as I know, she doesn't participate in any of his ventures, except very indirectly."

"How so? I sniffed around a little and I found no evidence she participated at all."

"I believe she's designed some pieces for a few boutiques he owns."

*Ah, used for money laundering, no doubt.* Assessing his sincerity, Nick inclined his head and stood. "The man I killed . . . any idea who he belongs to? The police can't ID him."

"None, but I'll ask a few questions if you'd like. He certainly took a shot at the wrong man. I wonder if he had any idea who you are."

"Oh, we'd met before. He knew. I'd appreciate it if you'd give me a call if you hear anything."

Denton's face had an amused expression. "I'd ask why you are so interested but I've met the lovely Reign. I assume you were in her bedroom for a reason. Is that why you didn't take the hit?"

Nick said mildly, "See, that's what I find so puzzling. How did you know I was approached in the first place?"

He heard Denton give a low laugh as he walked out the door.

It was almost impossible to park downtown on a Monday morning, so Nick had taken a cab, and now he hailed another one, wondering what to do next. Denton was a safe enough option. He gave the word "discreet" a whole new meaning, which was why he was so successful that he spent a great deal of time at his house in the Hamptons and vacationed in exotic places like Fiji and New Zealand. However, if Nick asked too many questions, especially in the wrong places, it would draw attention to the issue.

So how to handle it?

In his chosen profession, he was somewhat of a detective, which sounded incongruous given the purpose, but still held true. If he had a target, he needed to know—without anyone getting suspicious—everything he could about the subject. And he didn't have the advantage of a badge and people being obligated to talk to him either, so his methods were backhanded at times, but he usually got the job done.

The church was gray stone, the cemetery encircled by an iron fence that had rust spots. There was lichen on some of the headstones and many of the names were barely legible. Even in the city it still seemed peaceful. Nick paid the driver and walked up the steps swiftly, instinctively doing the holy cross once he entered the vestibule. He even took the time to kneel in front of the altar before he backtracked to his brother's office.

The door was open and he knocked lightly on the doorframe. "Busy?"

John was reading some document, but his gaze snapped up and his instant smile was genuine and nice to see. "Nick. Come on in."

There was no doubt they were brothers. Same dark wavy hair, same blue eyes, but John wore a white collar and dispensed counseling and salvation, and Nick dispensed something quite different.

"Glad you're alone." Nick took a chair, which

creaked ominously under his weight, and eyed the cluttered desk. "*Looks* like you're busy."

"Always."

"Don't give me the 'work of God is never done' speech or I'm out of here."

"We both know I don't bother to state the obvious, and your redemption is pretty dubious anyway. I haven't seen you in three months." There was reproof in John's voice. "I've left several messages and sent texts."

"Father, I have a confession, I've been busy. I've e-mailed about your financial portfolio."

"Funny." The papers were set aside. John's brows rose. "Doing?"

"The usual. Drugs, sex, rock and roll."

"Yeah, I don't believe the drugs, except you do like expensive bourbon. We both know you can't sing, but the sex part I'll buy." His brother voice was dry. "A truthful answer isn't necessary. Just a general overview is fine."

"I've been good. I visited Italy for a month. I just got back recently."

"Where?"

"Everywhere. Mom was fine. She's glad to be back in Sicily. I gained five pounds."

John laughed. "I'll bet. I always do." Then he sobered. "The visit? Necessity or vacation?"

That was about as direct a question Nick ever received about what he did for a living. "A bit of both," he answered evasively. "The world can be an unfriendly place now and then. Why is it the smell of being in a church makes me feel ten years old?"

"Come here more often and it might bring you into the present. I'm surprised the walls aren't bleeding. I sense your visit has a purpose."

He actually went to mass every single Sunday, but he wasn't about to reveal that bit of information. John was intuitive and would want to know why he didn't come to *this* church, and Nick didn't have a straightforward answer. He wasn't uncomfortable with his brother's vocation, he just didn't quite understand it.

"This has nothing to do with religion. You're intelligent. I want to pick your brain a little."

"Intelligent? What a compliment. I should hope I am, but we do come from the same parents, so maybe I am just fooling myself."

Nick couldn't help but laugh. "Okay, you win that round. Let me rephrase. There are not a lot of people I feel I can discuss matters with confidentially, but you are one of them. Besides, your specialty is to give advice and I think I might need some."

"So you are visiting the priest, not the brother?"

"I am visiting both, as it happens. People tend to think just because we bend the law now and then we aren't family-oriented people, and that is the worst misconception on this planet. I trust you. I'd trust you with my life."

"Let's hope that isn't an issue, but I'd protect you as well." John leaned back in his chair. "What is it?"

How to answer that one? Nick took a minute.

"How important is the truth if it frightens or hurts someone?"

"Is this pertinent or a just philosophical debate?" John's blue eyes were very direct.

"Pertinent." Nick thought about Reign. He said slowly, "I know someone in danger. I like this person, but explaining the situation might destroy our relationship."

"Relationship" might have been stretching it a little. One hot morning of wild sex was *not* a relationship.

"You seem to care about 'this person.'"

He did. Inexplicably. After one encounter? Usually with his lovers he was pretty detached. On purpose, but still detached. Nick muttered, "I don't want her hurt."

His brother, the priest, sat for a moment and seemed to reflect. "Her? So, a woman? What kind of danger is she in?"

"The bad kind."

John frowned, picking up a pen and rolling it in his long fingers. "Is it because of you?"

"Actually, no."

"That's a surprise, given what you do. Okay, so what exactly are you asking me?"

Nick ran his hand through his hair. "You know, I'm not sure. I'm having a small moral crisis. That's all. I know something she doesn't and I'm trying to decide if I should tell her or not."

"At the risk of sounding like a priest, can I mention that it is about time for the moral crisis?"

"No." The word came out as a growl.

"I think I'd like to meet this woman that has you, of all people, rattled."

No. His brother was a priest and Nick was . . . certainly not one. He was fairly sure Reign would find that amusing.

"I think *I* came here for advice, which I am not getting by the way."

"How will she handle it?"

When Nick thought back on the other night, he was able to say honestly, "She'll deal. That's how she operates. Straightforward and, though 'accepting' isn't the right word, she lives in this real world. Our world, to be specific."

"Our world? Mob wife?"

"Mob ex-wife. I don't sleep with married women, remember?"

"I've always admired that about you despite a few other flaws I have to overlook." John's smile was more of a boyish grin but he sobered quickly. "Nick, here is what I have to say. If you lose her through honesty, so be it. If you lose her because you said nothing, that will be very hard to live with, won't it?"

Nick rubbed his forehead. "You know, I had a feeling you were going to preach something exactly like that."

John slightly lifted his shoulders, his smile serene. "And when you walked through the door, I think you already knew the answer."

# SIX

He walked into the restaurant and heads turned.

Reign noted it as she sat at the table, smoothing the moisture on the side of her drink glass.

If she had to call it, the men recognized a dominant male when they saw one, and the women were just noticing a drop-dead gorgeous guy. Nick Fattelli leaned over to say something to the hostess and then focused his gaze in Reign's direction when the woman pointed.

The place was expensive. Men who threw their money around didn't do anything for her, but it wasn't a bad sign either that he'd picked somewhere nice. She wore a form-fitting sapphire dress and had picked lipstick just a little darker than her usual shade for contrast. His appreciative look told her the time she'd put into the decision was worth it.

"Hi, beautiful." Nick sat down and flashed white

teeth in that killer smile that had initially caught her attention.

He looked irritatingly refreshed and healthy, and she felt a little mowed over by her day in comparison. "Hi back."

It was like he went on full alert to her mood. "Did something happen?"

"No." She picked up her drink and took a sip. A little something *had* happened, but he wouldn't be interested in the nuances of her career. "All quiet on the Reign Supreme front. I've been staying with my sister until they replace the floor and closet doors and update my security system."

"Good." He had a slightly skeptical look on his face, but he seemed to accept she wasn't ready to talk about it.

He ordered a martini, not dirty but straight up with a twist of lemon, and when the waitress left, he told Reign, "I rarely drink gin, but the bartender doesn't know that. Hope it's top-shelf."

If the bartender had the slightest clue as to who he was serving, he'd take special care, of that she had no doubt. "I would think it would be impossible to ruin."

"It's the quality of the alcohol. Just like a beautiful woman. If she's physically attractive but spoiled, selfish, or even worse, unintelligent, no thanks. I like that dress, by the way."

"Thank you." She took a sip of her drink.

His gaze dropped deliberately to her cleavage. "No, thank *you*. Am I leering? I'm trying not to, but I'm pretty sure the effort is wasted."

It was odd how he could make her laugh, considering what she knew about him after checking with a few people who would have the information. He was freelance, not part of a particular family organization, but had a reputation for getting the job done swiftly and without any messy loose ends. Considering she'd seen him in action, she believed it. He was expensive, but thorough and professional. That faint accent she couldn't place must be a hint of Sicilian from his childhood, because he hadn't moved to the US until he was five, and he'd spent his childhood in Chicago.

Maybe they needed to get the conversation out of the way.

"Investment banker was a slight exaggeration, wasn't it?" she said, deliberately setting her drink down. "You have an office, I understand that, but I get the impression that isn't your primary occupation, which you know is what I've thought all along. It sounds to me like you inherited the family business."

His father, according to her source, had been one of the best, and Nick was reputedly even better.

Faster, smarter, and more deadly.

Why the hell she found him so fascinating, she wasn't sure, but maybe now she belonged to a rare and elite group of people in the world who could say a hit man saved their life.

The arrival of his drink negated her answer to that loaded question. Instead, after he took a drink, he said neutrally, "Top-shelf. Bombay Sapphire. Perfect." He set the glistening glass down. "The food here is supposed to be phenomenal. You're pretty fit—let's not forget I've seen every inch of you—so let me guess, fish or chicken?"

"We aren't going to talk about it?"

He regarded her over his glass, the crystal liquid glistening in the low lighting. "Reign, I think you ought to ask yourself how deep this conversation needs to go."

He had a point. She'd slept with him just once. Maybe she was making it too complicated too quickly.

*Back off.*

"Wrong. I'm a steak girl." Reign picked up her menu. "But I do skip the potatoes usually. I love them, but we all have to make choices in this life. I refuse to give up pasta. I know it is cliché among every Italian woman, but you should taste my lasagna."

Easy transition.

"Is that an invitation to dinner at your place soon? If so, I'm *in*."

He meant it, but in a sexual way. When he'd called, she'd known this evening was about seduction. It just figured, Reign thought in resignation, that the first man she'd been attracted to since Salvatore was also not right for her. In an entirely different way, of course, but definitely not a good choice.

There was quiet music playing in the background, something classical that she liked. Vivaldi's *The Four Seasons*. It sounded like it. The sophisticated atmosphere supported it.

The waitress returned—she seemed more attentive than normal, and Reign suspected it had a lot more to do with Nick than just good customer service. Young, brunette, and pretty, she took their order. Without asking, Nick ordered Reign a filet mignon with red wine sauce, medium rare, with a Caesar salad, and for himself a seared duck breast with risotto and roasted asparagus.

Reign didn't have much of a problem with men ordering for her, but she was amused by *his* choice.

"Duck?"

"I like duck." He shrugged those broad shoulders.

"I wouldn't have thought."

He set his elbows on the table. "Do I seem unsophisticated to you?"

Reign looked right back. "Apparently that boy from Sicily has some grown-up tastes."

There was immediate enlightenment in his eyes. "You have no idea. It seems like you might have been checking up on me."

"Would you respect me if I hadn't?"

"I suppose that's a good point. I'm a multifaceted man." He lightened that comment with an engaging grin. "They didn't serve a lot of duck when I was growing up, but hey, once I tasted it, I was hooked. How's that? What else do you want to know?"

The music changed: "Spring" to "Summer." A waiter passed by with a tray of food that smelled fantastic.

Her turn. Reign said frankly, "Everything."

"How about we go for partial knowledge and

explore it from there. Have I mentioned I like sex a lot?"

"I take it I might be enlightened soon."

"Is tonight good for you?"

Those azure eyes were a weakness for her. The way he looked at her caused an interesting flutter in the pit of her stomach. She picked up her drink. "Tonight is good. This must be the oddest way two people have ever started an affair I can think of."

"Maybe." Nick added in a devastatingly soft voice. "I've been thinking about you since the moment you walked out my door."

That was honest. Maybe more honest than she was willing to be, but she could give it a try. "I'm divorced and have a son."

One of the waitstaff arrived with a basket of bread and a dish of butter that held a hint of garlic. It smelled like heaven and also prevented him from commenting at once. He offered her the basket first. Then he said carefully, "We all have a past. If a person doesn't, they aren't even remotely interesting."

"I suppose that is one way to look at it."

"*Bella*, it is the only way to look at it."

"I take it you are *very* interesting, Mr. Fattelli?"

"I thought you wanted to call me Nicky."

"Is that an invitation?"

Dinner was delicious, and the aftermath promised to be more so.

Nick knew when a woman had pulled out all the stops—and Reign really had. Her dress was svelte and flattering, emphasizing that, yes, she had full breasts, but also a small waist and that nice ass. He had to wonder if she'd designed the garment just for her figure, because it fit perfectly, though she just wasn't tall enough to be one of those willowy runway models. When they'd left the restaurant, he'd known every single male there watched the sway of her hips as she walked by.

He did, that was for sure.

The matching pumps emphasized that her legs were athletic, and he'd found her lipstick bold but erotic.

This woman did something to him. He wasn't positive how he felt about it, but the impact was there.

"Sorry about the cab," he said as he waved one down. "I refuse to park my car down here unless it's necessary."

"Besides, you don't want your name to pop up in a police report again and you just had two drinks."

"That too." A yellow vehicle slid to the curb next to them, and he opened the door for her. "I always hedge my bets."

She got in and stretched out those gorgeous legs. "I suspect you do."

He slid in beside her and gave his address. She'd told him she liked his apartment when she'd stayed the other night. It was plain with leather couches and white walls, but punctuated by bursts of color from a few paintings of boats and the sea done by his cousin. They certainly weren't reproductions and lent the right flavor to the space. Austere, but at the same time bold and opulent, she'd said.

Not easy to achieve, and she knew something about style. More than he did, certainly.

When they pulled up to the building, he took her elbow and said hello to the doorman, guiding her to the elevator. The last time she'd been there was probably sort of a blur from the shock of the evening and the late hour, but this time she glanced around when he unlocked the door and commented, "This is nice. I remember it, but then again, I don't recall the details. That was an eventful night."

She swept the place with an assessing gaze. Terrific view of the city, big windows. . . . He paid a fortune in rent. The furnishings were minimal, but expensive, and while dark leather wouldn't be her choice, it suited him.

She turned and he said, "The next morning was better."

He dropped his keys on the table in the foyer. The clatter seemed very loud on the marble top. Nick smiled and said, "Take off your dress? A suggestion, not an order, and the heels can stay on in my opinion."

Lucky for him, Reign was on board but had conditions, as usual. "I don't take orders, you already know that. I'll take it off, but then you're naked on the bed. How is that for a compromise?"

"Give me a show?"

Those emerald eyes held a sultry look. "I'm not a stripper, but I'll do my best."

Nick reached out and touched her chin. It was just a brush. "I'm really looking forward to this, and for the record, I don't visit strip clubs. Just improvise. I suspect you'll do just fine."

She glanced directly at his crotch. "I get that you kind of like the idea."

His erection *was* uncomfortable, but then again, she just had that effect on him in general. "Reign, can we please just go into the bedroom?"

She swung around in a swirl of dark hair and glanced over her shoulder. "You have no idea how lucky you are that you put 'please' in that sentence."

He had some idea about two seconds later, when that beautiful dress slipped down and she stepped out of it. It landed in a pool of blue fabric on the floor and underneath he discovered she wore a lacy black bra and a thong. He'd follow that ass to the end of the earth, he thought as he walked behind her, enjoying the view.

Bra next. He caught it as she tossed it over her shoulder, and he really, really wished he could see the movement of those fabulous tits as she walked, but the view was sexy enough with her heels and just that tiny black thong.

Then she stopped and bent over in the doorway of his bedroom, gliding her underwear down her hips and the length of her legs. Nick had managed quite a number of situations that required precise control, but he almost lost it right then and there, especially since he was fairly sure she'd prolonged it on purpose just to taunt him.

Heels only, she turned to face him. Those generous breasts were tight—yes, she was enjoying this too—and quivered just a fraction with each breath, betraying her excitement. "So?"

"So what?" Like a seasoned predator, he came into the room and reached for her. He was bigger, faster, deadlier. . . .

"Don't touch me." She evaded him, and sexy as hell—beyond even his vivid imagination—she stood there in just those stiletto heels and narrowed her emerald eyes. "Not until you take your clothes off. Wasn't that the deal?"

"I don't make deals." Nick reached for her again.

"You keep your word with *me*."

He stopped. There was a part of him that understood that certain equations added up to something that was more important to one person more than the other. This was apparently important to her.

So he'd obey her rules.

He caressed her shoulders, but then removed his hands and lifted them in the air in a gesture of surrender. "I do think I promised that."

"Off, Mr. Fattelli. Strip for me. You won't regret it."

His suit coat hit the floor. "I'm going to hold you to that."

"Are we in some sort of hurry?" Naked and evidently in charge, she smiled and cupped her breasts, lifting them a little in her palms. "I thought you wanted to watch me give you a little entertainment."

Damn it, he couldn't get the buttons undone on his shirt with her touching herself like that, his fingers suddenly clumsy. Finally he stripped out of it and tossed it aside, and then unfastened his belt. "Keep going, sweetheart."

She licked her lips provocatively. "Not until I see that big cock of yours."

"I'm working on that." He unzipped his fly and stepped out of his tailored slacks. To say he had an erection was an understatement..

"That looks very . . . *interesting*." She purred out the last word. "Lie down."

Nick moved to the bed because that's what she'd said she wanted, and he reclined against the headboard, lifting his brows. "Don't stop now."

"I have no intention of stopping." She brushed her nipples with her fingers, which was quite a sight. She had such a lush body. Reign asked him directly, still holding her breasts and absolutely knowing what she was doing to him, "I take it you like what you see?"

"Hell yes." That was not a lie.

"Hmm. How often do you . . . well . . . how do I put this? Jerk off?"

He drawled with more nonchalance than he felt, "That's kind of a personal question, Ms. Grazi, but I'm willing to answer it. I'm going to say it happens fairly often if I am not involved with anyone at the time. I'm a guy."

She looked like a wet dream in those heels and nothing else. When she slid her hand slowly down the plane of her stomach and cupped it erotically between her legs, he had to stifle a groan. She said in a very sexy low tone, "Women do it too, you know."

# SEVEN

S he was playing with fire.

Reign knew it.

Nick looked gorgeous in a purely masculine way lying there in his aroused state, his gaze focused on her every movement, his rangy body supine but hardly relaxed.

Not with that prominent hard-on.

His bedroom had the same view as the rest of the apartment. City lights everywhere, the sleek lines of skyscrapers, and the drop to the streets below.

"Masturbate?" He was obviously on board because his voice was just a little uneven. His bedroom had several retro posters and shining wood floors. The bed took up a lot of the loft space, but the rest of the furnishings were actually fairly sparse, which she liked. "Show me."

He'd certainly been intent when she'd touched her breasts.

At the moment, he was *riveted*.

"Uhm . . . yes." She lightly rotated her fingers, stimulating her clit as she stood there in her just her heels. Her head tilted back and she felt the sensuous brush of her hair on her bare back. "Feels good."

"I think I might be able to help you out even better."

"Haven't you heard, Nicky, no one knows what you like more than *you* do? Just the right pressure and touch and . . . oh." Sensation rippled through her body even as she spoke.

His voice was low and commanding. "Reign, come here. You're driving me crazy on purpose and I think it's over."

All her life she'd dealt with dominant men and she knew that tone well. Independence was important to her, but picking her battles was always wise. It didn't hurt that she was just as interested as he was in what was going to happen next, and he was dead serious. If she didn't comply, he was coming to get her, so she might as well keep as much control over the situation as possible.

She approached the bed. "You have something specific in mind?"

"Those beautiful tits. My mouth."

"That's pretty specific."

"Bring them over and I'll be a happy man."

Reign crawled on top of him. "I like this position."

As she straddled his hips, his fingers lightly stroked first her hips and then the sensitive undersides of her breasts while she lightly rubbed her sex against his erection. His heavy-lidded eyes held her gaze. "Yeah. I like it too."

Reign knew he could feel she was really wet and slick. "I should take my shoes off. They might tear the sheets."

"No way." He guided her up and down his hard length, encouraging the motion. "I like the shoes and I can afford new sheets."

"Fantasy is fine, but—"

"Leave them on."

"Yes, sir." Reign grinned and ran the tip of her heel up his calf. It had to hurt at least a little.

"I need to be inside you." He abruptly rolled her over, his breath warm against her lips, a lock of dark hair over his forehead. "I'm talking you have *no* idea how bad I need to be inside you."

"Go for it," she challenged because she was pretty on the edge as well. "Fuck me."

Instead he kissed her, long but hard and fairly graphic about what he wanted. His tongue delved deep and then her knees were apart and he entered her so abruptly she caught her breath.

Immediately he lifted his head, concern in those pure blue eyes. "Okay? Did I hurt you?"

There was no doubt she was playing fast and loose with a man without rules, but he seemed at least intent on keeping the illusion going so she didn't need to be afraid of him.

"We're good." She nipped at his shoulder, maybe even drawing a little blood from the salty taste. "Don't stop now."

"I'm not sure I could." He sounded like he meant

it even as he loomed over her, his mouth teasing her throat.

It was a disturbing thought that his intellect intrigued her, his open sensual appeal aside. She normally considered herself a very self-aware person. With her background, she needed to be. Nick Fattelli broke quite a few of her rules.

He began to move, thrusting in and out, the penetration urgent and possessive, and Reign moved with him, their bodies in an instinctive carnal rhythm that was so natural even in the haze of pleasure she noticed how well they matched each other.

He was dangerous in more than one way. Not just to her person, but to her peace of mind.

Deadly, even.

How could she possibly feel safe?

"Babe." His lips touched hers as he withdrew and slid in again. "God, it's good."

It was. Reign was getting close, the tension moving her higher and higher. Her thighs tightened around his hips. She pulled him closer. "Kiss me again."

He did, and she kissed him back, her nails raking his shoulders as it started to happen, her eyes closing as the pleasure crested and she sank beneath the tidal wave. As she came he reacted, his cry just strangled enough she registered it even though she was lost, floating, her body trembling. Her breath was caught somewhere in her throat.

Eventually, she drifted back into the moment and realized he was moving his fingers in an idle pattern on her inner thigh, a slight smile on his face. He asked, "Hi? You with me again?"

"That was—"

"Incredible?" He licked her right nipple. "I agree." Poised over her, he was all male grace and power, and though she knew he'd climaxed because she'd felt the powerful pulse of his release, he was still impressively rigid.

"I was going to say adequate." There was a laugh in her voice.

"You pushing me? *Me?*"

She was. And it was unwise, but still exciting, and maybe she should retreat rather than advance.

Actually she'd never been all that good at backing off.

"We've only been to bed twice."

"But had sex how many times?"

He had a point. Reign laughed. "Okay, you win there, Nicky."

His fingers touched her hair and then her face, before trailing lower, and his voice was serious. "I really think you're beautiful."

"I've been told that before."

"How often?"

He looked pretty cute jealous. She couldn't help but smile. "I don't keep a log or anything. And believe it or not, I don't sleep around. I've been burned once. Never again."

"What does that mean? Anyone ever hurt you? I'll kill him."

It was so much part of the world she lived in that she believed him. "No." She pressed her fingers to his mouth. "Not the way you mean. Not physically. My ex-husband was not the man I thought he was, but I'm over it—and him. That bastard will probably screw up and end up dead, but he is my son's father and I want no part of what happens to him, all right? Let him fuck up his own life, but I'm not interested in explaining his mistakes to my child. My father would have taken care of it a long time ago but I asked him to back off. Ray was *my* problem."

"Are you extracting some sort of assurance from me?"

"If I did, would you honor it?"

His brows shot up. "Are you asking me if you can rely on my word? Reign, if there is anything on this planet that you can count on, it is that if I give you my word, I'll follow through. However, if I don't promise, there's a reason and all bets are off."

She rubbed his bare chest and shifted so her thigh draped suggestively over his. "I believe that. But I'm more interested in earthy pursuits than revenge right now."

"You aren't scared?"

She stopped, lashes dropping, and rested her forehead on his shoulder. "I'm terrified. What the fuck do you think?"

Her body was like some sort of drug. Nick knew he'd never been so hungry for a woman before, but then again, it wasn't just the sex.

*Problem one.*

It was dark and the air-conditioning hummed in

the background. The bed was soft, the city lights giving them a gentle glow behind the shade at the big window, and he stroked her arm in long, slow motions with his hand.

He wanted her again, and she rested against him in a languid pose of submission, but he knew if he tried to take anything before she was ready, he'd have an argument on his hands.

*Problem two.*

"Talk to me about it."

"No."

"Reign, you know you have to."

"No."

"You smell like flowers." He licked her earlobe.

"That's shampoo." She laughed, but pushed him away with a light shove he ignored. "Give me a minute."

"I think you'd go again right now." He curved her into him, positioning their bodies, his arms bringing her closer. "But instead talk to me?"

"I don't know what to say. I can't think of a single reason that man was in my bedroom. Not one."

He could. It bothered him.

He needed to think, and this was just not the time, not when his whole body was on fire. "We'll think about it later. Agreed?"

"Are you always hard?" She was laughing, but when he entered her she went quiet and sighed and her arms encircled his neck. Her breasts were taut and her nipples erect. "Nicky."

"Feels good?"

"You tell me."

If he was inclined to be honest—and he wasn't—he might have mentioned that this was more his speed, as he moved inside her gently and easily, since they'd already made love twice.

*Problem three.*

Heaven on earth took on a new meaning. He really liked sex. Like really, really liked it. But she was exceptional. Just the light touch of her palms on his back turned him on.

He didn't want exceptional. He wanted the typical sexual encounter that was just a blip on his screen. It made things easier.

In short, it felt too good.

"You like me here." He pushed deep on purpose.

"Pretty much." She arched in response. "Don't stop now."

"Jesus, Reign." He was starting, on such short acquaintance, to believe that to be true.

"At the moment, I'm pretty sure you feel that way. You just want to fuck me."

And outspoken. "I *am* fucking you."

"See?" Long dark lashes lowered over her eyes. "Uhm. And I like it."

*Problem four.*

He found her honesty and her sense of humor almost as appealing as her beauty, and that was saying something. "I'm not *just* fucking you."

Oh hell, not a good admission.

Even as he thought about amending that declaration, to his relief, Reign said, "If you make this complicated, I'll never speak to you again."

*Great, another problem.* Was this problem five? He could tell she didn't want him interfering in her life.

"Is that an ultimatum?" His voice was raspy, but he asked anyway.

"I know what you are. . . . I can't think about this too much."

"What am I?" He stopped. It took some self-control, but he went still, inside her but not moving, looking into those amazing emerald eyes as they opened in question at the pause.

"The single worst decision I could make is if I respond to that question. Don't stop."

"Reign—"

"I'm serious, Nicky."

It wasn't as if he didn't completely understand, even though he was a man. There was a vulnerability to her slender form, and the implicit trust she gave just letting him even touch her, that moved him.

He finished it with long measured strokes, taking them both where they wanted to go, his hands sliding beneath her to lift her into each heated thrust. Reign wasn't shy about being vocal in her enjoyment, and his own climax was a shattering event that left him sheened with sweat and confirmed his heart was in good shape anyway.

Afterward there was nothing but measured breathing as they recovered, sprawled across the sheets.

*I know what you are. . . .*

Still entwined intimately, he wondered if he should withdraw, but decided *fuck* that. His cock liked it exactly where it was. He did give her the courtesy of lifting his weight off, but even on his elbows those spectacular breasts pressed his chest. "What am I?"

"Persistent, apparently." She sounded breathless.

"Guilty as charged. Just tell me what you meant."

Any other woman might have equivocated, but not Reign.

She looked up at him and brushed his hair back. "Oh, fuck, you aren't going to back off, are you? My entire life my father has warned me about men like you."

"My entire life, my mother has warned me about women like you." He kissed her right breast, savoring the supple fullness of her nipple. "Be careful of the ones who wear heels and nothing else."

"That was your idea."

She liked it when he licked the underside of her breast. Definitely. It was sublime. . . .

"Stop that. I'm serious." She lightly slapped his back and laughed.

"Hey, I like *that,* hit me again." He caught her wrists. "I need a good spanking."

"Nicky."

"Reign." He kissed her and pressed her to the pillows holding her arms above her head. Then he told her without loosening his grip, "This isn't just about how much I like you in bed. I think you are the most striking woman I have ever met, and it isn't just your looks. You have . . . a heart."

"How could you possibly know me well enough—"

"Shit, I *know*. Stay the night?"

"I've slept here before."

"That was different. I insisted." He moved a little, just adjusting their position. "I'm very good at not letting other people make choices, because it all has to be done so fast usually, but not all of life has to be at lightning speed. I want it to be your choice tonight."

It was sobering to realize that was about as far out on a limb as he'd ever gone for a woman. Ever. Not that he'd never discussed it with his other lovers, but he certainly had not issued that humble invitation. Sex had been the goal, not sharing his bed.

Front and center, he wanted her to stay.

"Sleep with me?" Never in his life had he asked in that tone. *Not just with my dick but with* me.

He would never say it out loud, but he felt it, as the request was held there suspended between them.

Reign touched his face. "I'd love to, but you have to promise I'll regret it in the morning."

It eased the moment.

There was a reason he really was attracted to this woman. He kissed her again before he answered. "Oh yeah, I'll be very bad. Maybe you should take a moment and write up a list of what you won't do."

"Now you're making it an invitation I can't refuse."

"I could just tie you up and you'd have no choice."

"Uhm." She wriggled closer. "A little bondage sounds promising. What else? Torture me by withholding sex?"

"I doubt that." He didn't genuinely smile often, but he did then.

Her guard slipped for just a moment. "I wish I didn't like you."

"You know, I was just thinking the same thing about you."

# EIGHT

The yacht wasn't his preference, but Salvatore did join in now and again, just to please his mother.

It was a lovely vessel. Sleek, expensive, and fast.

Kind of, he thought irreverently, like his mother. She wouldn't like the comparison, but it slipped into his mind just the same. His parents had an understanding about fidelity that they seemed comfortable with, but it would never be part of *his* marriage.

If he ever got married. Not that long ago he'd been out shopping for rings, but maybe, he'd decided in retrospect, he'd been seeing the dream through so he could face the reality.

Reign wasn't ever going to marry him.

"Thanks," he said to one of the waiters as he accepted some champagne. "Don't be a stranger." The wind tickled his hair and smelled a lot like the bay, with just a hint of maybe some ocean out there.

Nice moon, lovely women, good booze . . . he was fairly miserable.

Go figure.

"Yes, sir." The young man left with a slight smile.

*Yeah, go ahead and laugh. . . . I'd find it funny, too, but it's my life. . . .*

"Sal."

He turned, flute in hand. The woman who joined him was young and very beautiful. She wore a bathing suit, was barefoot, and her fair hair was windblown. He said pleasantly, "Carmen."

"I asked if you were coming." She smiled over the rim of her glass. A cosmopolitan, if he had to guess. If he remembered correctly, she liked them with vanilla vodka and cranberry juice, but then again, it had been a while.

Still, she looked great. Flat stomach, store-bought tits, but . . . almost every single woman on the boat had those if he was a judge of the crowd, and his problem had always been complexity. He never wanted just an easy lay.

Carmen Dolce's interest involved a horizontal surface. He'd known that for years now. Had he wanted to accept the offer, he might now be the son-in-law of a very influential man.

"My mother's parties aren't always my favorite." Sal's comment was offhand.

Carmen took a sip—a very big sip—from her glass. Her blond hair brushed her breasts. If everything was different, he might have gotten sucked into the vortex. Maybe he should be grateful to

Reign for rejecting him. She stared at him. "Why not?"

Now see, this was why they hadn't communicated all that well in the past. He said, "It seems to always be a bunch of people with too much time on their hands and too much money, all getting drunk together."

"I seem to notice *you're* drinking." Carmen gestured with her glass and some of the liquid inside splashed on her bare toes, which made her give a small squeal of laughter.

"Yeah," he agreed dryly. "Self-preservation. Who can blame me?"

Then he saw her. Just a casual movement out of the corner of his eye, but he realized who it was and for a moment froze with his drink halfway to his mouth, as he turned to look at a group of people gathered on the deck.

*Reign* was on his parents' boat?

No way.

She looked beautiful too, in some sort of sarong-style dress she'd probably designed herself, the tropical colors complementing her long, sleek dark hair, and the breeze rippling the fabric against her body, accentuating those eye-catching curves.

But really, as much as he appreciated the view, what the hell was she doing there? Considering the enmity between their families, it seemed like a very unusual choice for her to make, and even more perplexing that his mother had invited her.

"Who are you staring at?" Carmen followed his

gaze and narrowed her eyes. "Oh yeah. I think I'm getting it. I take it you know Reign Grazi."

Maybe Carmen was more intelligent than he gave her credit for. Well, she probably was, since he didn't give her much credit at all and she still managed somehow to get into Columbia. Of course, that could have been due to her influential father. Sal murmured in confirmation, "I do know Reign."

*Biblically,* he could have added, but that wasn't anyone's business besides theirs. "Our families just don't get along too well, so I was startled to see her here."

"Know her?" Even Carmen lifted her perfectly plucked brows. "That's putting it mildly. I think she came with the tall, dark-haired guy. He's not exactly new in town, but he's not from right here either. Word has it Chicago. Nick something. He's pretty cute."

*Oh perfect.*

Sal leaned against the railing. At least it was a pleasant night and the salt air was refreshing. He needed to keep that in mind. There were worse things in this world than being on a yacht with pretty girls and expensive booze.

Like his ex-lover coming to a family party with her new lover.

There *was* a man standing next to Reign. It wasn't that he was even touching her, but he had a possessive air and occasionally leaned in close to say something—much closer than anyone would normally dare if there wasn't a sexual relationship. Sal understood body language and in particular understood Reign.

Whoever the man was, they were definitely sleeping together.

Apparently this night wasn't going to improve. She would never allow that much of an intrusion in her personal space if they weren't intimate.

"I need to go change." Carmen said it with a hint of challenge in her voice. "I put my clothes in the stateroom. Care to come . . . *help* me?"

Sal tried to switch his focus, but it wasn't easy.

It was ridiculous that he was affronted over Reign showing up with this guy. He was going to guess it was Nick Fattelli, the man who'd shot the hit man in her bedroom, and he looked the part. Tall, muscular, well dressed, confident in how he moved, and the asshole had definitely some connections or Sal's mother wouldn't have invited him in the first place. . . .

*Bastard.*

"Hey?"

Sal finally swept his unfocused gaze to Carmen. She'd already untied the top of her suit and though maybe everyone couldn't see it, he sure had a nice view of those enhanced tits. They were very tanned too, as if she sunbathed with her top off often. Nice and round and within reach—38D if he was a judge.

"Sure," he said recklessly, because he was hurt. Whether it was warranted or not, he *was* disillusioned, and there was a reason "on the rebound" was a catchphrase. Seeing Reign with someone else sliced like a knife. "I'd love to help."

"Show me the way?"

*Right.* Stateroom. Sure. Like it was complicated, and if she'd left her clothes there she knew just where it was, but fine. He knew an invitation when he heard one.

Below deck there were actually three small staterooms—his parents had quite a lot of money, and this was a very nice boat—and a galley, right now bustling with staff getting out the canapés for the guests. Sal led her to the one he used if they were out for longer than just a day and held the door for her. His mother had excellent taste, and it was furnished with mahogany to match the built-in bed. The bedspread was masculine with blue and yellow stripes, and there were several nautical pictures of old sailing vessels on the walls.

"I've always wanted to do it with you." Carmen ran her hand over his shirt and dropped her top completely. "But you never would. We've known each other for how many years? I did everything to catch your attention."

*"Do it." Yeah, that was romantic.*

"When I met you, you were still in high school. In some states that's statutory rape," Sal said dryly, "especially if the male is seven years older."

"I'm not sixteen now." Her brows arched and she pressed against him, her arms coming around his neck. "I wasn't a virgin even then. I know what I'm doing. Kiss me."

He did. She tasted like the cosmopolitan, and her

bare back was warm and smooth, her breasts pressed against his chest. . . . And he felt . . . nothing.

She didn't have silky ebony hair and a sultry smile and green eyes.

Goddamnit, he needed to get over it, but he obviously wasn't since he was kissing another woman, a beautiful sexy young coed, and still thinking about Reign.

This was all wrong. Not fair to her, or for that matter, to him.

*Stop it now.*

Gently, he disengaged himself. "Carmen, you know what, I still can't do this. You are a gorgeous girl and I'm tempted, trust me, but I'd be using you and I don't do that to women. I like you. We're friends. I think we'd better leave it right there for now. I'm involved with someone else and while this wouldn't precisely be cheating, it feels like it to me."

He felt guilty for the anger and disappointment in her eyes, but knew it was nothing compared to how he'd feel if he had meaningless sex with her. Not that he was a saint or anything—hell no, he was going to law school so he could help out family and friends when they needed a little legal assistance and advice because their world was his world too—but he did have his own moral code.

"Do your parents realize it's Reign Grazi?" Carmen snatched her top back off the floor of the stateroom, her voice tinged with a hint of venom. "Because I'd bet they wouldn't be happy about it."

Yes, Carmen was definitely smarter than he'd thought previous to this moment. Obviously she'd seen his expression when he'd spotted Reign and her date.

*Hell hath no fury like a woman scorned. . . .*

"They don't have to be happy," he said quietly. "I'm a grown man and get to make my own decisions."

That smacked of an open admission, but then again, he'd never been the one to want to keep the affair quiet in the first place.

"Affair." He despised that word. "Involvement," "relationship"—both were much better. However, he understood Reign was a little older than him, and she had a son to consider, and so he'd honored her request they keep it low on the radar.

Carmen said in a voice far too jaded for someone her age, "If you think that's true, you're just fooling yourself, Sal," as she hooked her bathing suit top between her breasts.

"You could be right," he responded. "I wonder about that myself all the time."

Reign should have asked more questions.

An evening sail and drinks on the yacht of a friend?

That had sounded harmless, and she'd been persuaded to come along, only since Vince was still on Long Island, and truthfully, she didn't go out enough.

The pertinent information omitted, though, had been that it was Sal's family party. To say her former lover's mother was able to be gracious under pressure was an understatement, because Reign had seen the unguarded look on the woman's face when she realized just who Nick had brought along. But Mrs. Ariano had recovered fairly quickly and at least greeted her with cool cordiality.

In his defense, Nick was probably unaware of the tension between their families, though with him it was always hard to tell. Reign gave him a sidelong glance and guessed that maybe he knew it now, if he didn't before. When Sal approached—and she'd known he would sooner or later the moment she realized he was also on board—with his good-looking face set, his sailing clothes a casual navy shirt that suited his blond hair and khaki shorts, Nick looked more bland than usual.

If he'd invited her just to flaunt their relationship to Sal, she'd strangle him.

"Sal," she said neutrally.

"Reign. You look amazing, as always." He took both her hands and kissed her. On the cheek, but it was still nice and conjured images of the nights they'd spent together. . . . And when his hands touched her shoulders and he squeezed a little, it evoked memories that were probably better left behind.

*No.*

Somehow, as he matured, Salvatore had managed to keep a modicum of idealism that she found charming, and he was very nice in bed—*very nice*—but their problem was he claimed he loved her.

Deal-breaker.

It wasn't that there was no trust left in her. Sure

there was. She trusted her parents. She trusted her sister, and of course she trusted her son. Otherwise, she was somewhat cautious thanks to her ex-husband.

"Thank you," she murmured.

"Having a good time?" Sal wasn't quite as good as Nick in hiding his feelings. Though she'd always been sure he'd make an excellent lawyer, since he was smart and articulate, he wasn't exactly transparent, but close.

One of the things she really liked about him—she'd always known where she stood.

Why did life have to be *so* difficult?

"Fattelli." Nick offered his hand. A boat cruised by and he had to raise his voice a little to be heard over the engine.

"Nice to meet you." Sal took his hand and they shook, but if Reign had to call it, it was more like two generals weighing the strength of their opposing armies than a friendly meeting.

If she was the prize, they could just get over it. "To sum it up, Sal and I are old friends," Reign said after taking a sip of champagne. "But our fathers are not."

"I guess that explains the hint of hostility in the air." Nick was drinking scotch and the double meaning didn't escape any of them.

"If I had known who was hosting the party, I'd have declined." Reign turned her face to the breeze coming off the ocean. The city looked gorgeous in the distance, and light danced off the waves. It felt lovely on deck: cool and light. She could feel both men watching her hair ripple across her shoulders. "I'd appreciate it, Sal, if you'd tell your mother that. I didn't come to make her uncomfortable."

"We shouldn't inherit the sins of our fathers."

It was Nick who said, "Oh, but we do. Figuratively and literally."

An interesting comment. She didn't know enough about his background. Reign studied the planes and shadows of Nick's face in the starlight. "I think that maybe you speak from experience."

"No comment." He turned. "I wouldn't mind another drink. Can I get either of you anything?"

Sal said with only the slightest sardonic undertone, "I'll take a martini straight up with a twist."

"We have similar tastes obviously." Nick turned to her. "Johnnie Black?"

"Thank you."

Both of them watched him walk away, not speaking, and then Sal leaned against the rail, his body taut. "This is really awkward. I feel like I should apologize, but then again, I am not sure for what."

"We are in the same boat."

They both laughed then, and it was spontaneous and felt good. He'd always had a very engaging grin. "I suppose we are. Literally."

"I didn't mean it that way." The other boat had turned and cruised by again, someone on the deck raising his glass at them. She gave a halfhearted wave back.

"I still love you," Sal said.

*Oh shit.* She didn't need this conversation, but she'd seen him when he'd realized she was there.

He'd been stricken, exposed, his reaction naked on his face.

And if only Sal didn't have an emotional commitment to their relationship she couldn't handle, everything might be different.

The drink could not come soon enough. "If you didn't we'd be together."

He caught her arm, his fingers tightening. "Reign, what the fuck is wrong with you? I *love* you. Explain how I am supposed to apologize for that?"

"I don't want you to apologize and I can't really explain it. I just need to walk away."

"If you think that helps," he said bitterly, looking impossibly handsome as he stood there. "Think again."

"What about the beautiful blonde all over you?"

He looked away. "You might notice I'm here with you instead."

Inwardly, she winced. For him. For them both. "If you think this is easy for me, think again. I . . . I can't . . ."

"Commit. I know." He finished the sentence for her, his smile bleak. "You know when I first saw you here, I thought—"

There was a small sound like a pop and his entire body jerked.

The bullet caught him in the shoulder. Sal looked more surprised than anything, his hand going to the small hole that appeared in his shirt like he was trying to figure out what happened. Then the second shot got him in the abdomen, making him stumble backward.

*What the hell?*

Just as astounded, Reign stood there in shock for one horrifying moment until she was knocked flat, her glass flying out of her hand, the wind leaving her lungs, and she felt like a little kid who lost it on the swing set at recess. Nick was the one to push her down apparently since he said fiercely in her ear, "I apologize for spilling your drink but I think we have something a little complicated going on here. Don't—and I mean it—move."

Then he got up and left her.

# NINE

All fucking hell had broken loose. Somewhere a woman was screaming, and the deck cleared like magic as well-dressed guests scattered.

The first thing Nick did was the logical reaction. He tried to figure out where the gunfire was coming from. He crawled along the deck, hoping Reign obeyed—for once—and peered out over the water. It made no sense to fire on a boat where you could be easily apprehended, so it must have come from a second craft.

*Bingo.*

The small boat was heading across the harbor fast, directly away from them. He would have opened fire back, but it was too far gone by now for any accuracy and he just wasn't sure. Yes, he'd killed a few men in his life, but never unless he was *sure*.

Random drive-by boating attack? He doubted it. They'd been after Reign.

He stood, his Glock hanging at his side, and walked back, only to find Reign hadn't exactly followed his directions and was on her knees next to Ariano. "Give me your shirt," she said with impressive calm considering the tears streaming down her face. "Right now, Fattelli, and if you hesitate one second, I'll just kill you and take it off of you."

She sounded pretty sincere.

"Let's not get bloodthirsty. The shirt is yours." He dropped his jacket and did just what she asked, unbuttoning and handing over the object she requested. By now people were timidly emerging from different places, because gunfire was like flushing quail with this elegant crowd, which, he thought as he watched people peer around corners, was ironic.

It wasn't like he'd never been in this position before. He bent over Ariano, who was going into shock, and he didn't need to be a physician to see that. "The shoulder is nothing," he said like a surgeon doing triage, but he'd seen more than his share of wounded men. "That belly shot might have hit vitals. Let's get this boat turned around. I think the party is over now anyway."

"You were the one invited." Reign knelt there with her dark hair in a shining curtain, blood pooling around her knees. "The boat. Good idea. Make it happen. His mother won't really want to talk to me, especially now if this is my fault. Besides, I'm staying with him. Go."

Interesting that she also realized she was the target. Or maybe not *that* interesting, since a man was shot in her home only a few days ago.

Nick went. He tried to keep a low profile along the deck in case he was wrong about the retreating boat, racing, shirtless, finding his hostess after a few inquiries, letting her know it was her son that had been shot.

They were back at the port with impressive speed, and luckily, between Reign's efforts and a doctor on board who was one of the guests, there was an ambulance waiting when they docked and Ariano seemed to be holding his own. Awake and lucid, he almost seemed more concerned with Reign's distress than his injuries. Bloody and weak, he was strapped to a gurney, and Nick had to give credit to the response time of the nearest hospital.

Those swirling red lights did nothing to improve the situation, and Reign truly did look stricken.

"I'll be fine," Ariano promised, holding her hand, though it was a little hard to believe considering he was covered in blood and pale as a ghost. "Stop crying. You never cry."

The victim's mother rushed up in her expensive black cocktail dress, but the EMT ignored her and asked Reign, "Are you his wife? You're awfully pale. If you'd care to ride along—"

Reign shook her head, standing up. "We are just very good friends."

It was true, her pallor nearly matched his.

Ariano actually joked. "She won't say yes."

When the gurney was loaded into the ambulance and Reign turned to Nick, he said evenly before she could speak, "I know. We're going to the hospital. I'll drive you there and stay as long as you need me."

"Thank you." Her voice was hushed.

"Like I'd leave you alone, especially after this particular evening." Nick took her arm, steering her back toward where he'd parked his car in a bevy of expensive vehicles on the pier. "Come on. He's going to be in surgery for a while; you do know that, right? Did you eat anything at all?"

Reign shook her head again. How she managed to look beautiful with smudged mascara, he didn't know, but somehow she pulled it off. "There's no way I could eat now, I—"

"Yes, there is. It's a mistake to forget that a human being must eat and sleep to stay strong. We're going to stop somewhere and talk about this, and then we'll go to the hospital and find out how he's doing, okay? The bottom line here is there's nothing you can do for him until he's out of recovery. If you can argue that point, go ahead and give it a try."

"There's blood on the hem of my dress."

"No one will notice. I'll pick someplace dark." He pressed a button on his keychain. "If this is going to be a long night, you're not going through it on no fuel. Stop arguing with me."

The first hint of humor surfaced. "Does it work for anyone? Arguing with you?"

"Nope." He opened her door. "Or at least not in their favor. Get in."

She slid into the car and settled into the seat. Typically Reign, she rallied enough to lift her head and say, "I'm letting you get away with ordering me around."

"Yeah, let's talk about your independence later."

"Here we go, arguing again."

He actually admired her firm determination to take care of herself, but the situation, especially after the events of this evening, had him worried. Nick hated being in the dark—the convoluted way he'd been approached to take the hit on her had given him pause at the time, and now he was more confused than ever over what exactly was happening. He got in the driver's seat and started the car, trying to make sure he didn't look uneasy, but he was.

He could have sworn they weren't followed to the pier earlier.

It was instinct to pay attention to any car that seemed to be consistently going the same direction. None had, or else it had been done so skillfully he hadn't caught it, and that was unlikely.

What did it mean?

Not sure.

Maybe her cell phone had a passenger. The evolution of tracking devices was ongoing, and he had contacts that kept up with the latest, but there was always something brewing in yet another devious brain.

He chose a pizza place that was appropriately casual a few blocks from the hospital and ushered her inside. Without being obvious, he tried to decipher her expression. Then he ordered a carafe of Chianti and a pepperoni, black olive, and green pepper pizza without asking what she preferred, because he was pretty sure she didn't care. He waited until the waiter brought the glasses and their wine before saying anything to her.

She still looked stricken but not quite so shell-shocked. Nick poured her a glass, handed it over, and asked succinctly, "Can we go over this again? Who wants you dead?"

The man had a way with words.

A very straightforward way.

Reign was willing to go out on a limb and say a date with Nick Fattelli was pretty much an adventure every single time.

The restaurant was quiet and low-key, and it smelled of oregano and Parmesan. She was still shaken from the shooting and had to consciously take a deep breath before she picked up her wine-glass. "I don't know."

At least the wine was smooth and mellow. Good choice. Her hand shook just a little, and some wine splashed out, but otherwise she thought she'd been pretty calm, considering.

She said carefully, "They shot Sal."

The booth was actually very comfortable, even if it was hardly the most upscale place, and the juke-box in the corner was playing some sort of oldie. But she felt safe, and that was pretty important at the moment. Only because Nick was there, and maybe that was an illusion. This man sitting across the table, who was he? Complex, that was certain. Safe? Debatable.

"Oh yeah, they did." Nick would never be a man to deal with less than the stark truth, she'd known that the moment she met him. "But, given what happened the night we met, do we both agree they were probably aiming for you? It takes some skill to shoot from a moving boat. They missed. He lost. They could have been gunning for you. I am not sure how often it happens in your life, but the sudden frequency of flying bullets your direction does send up flags."

As if she didn't already feel incredibly guilty. Sal had lost, but hopefully not his life. "You've shot at someone from a moving boat, Fattelli?"

"I've done a number of interesting things." He sat back, wineglass in hand, his face shadowed. "It's been established you know what I stand for."

The closest he'd come to admitting it.

"Assassin?"

"Hey, let's not get sophisticated. I've never said that."

"Oh, I beg your pardon."

In the end Nick was faintly amused. She could see it even in the inadequate light of the fake stained-glass fixtures. "Look, as awful as the evening turned out, I'm not actually involved in all of this. Don't blame me."

He had a point. Nick had been helpful, calm, and in command. Good man in a crisis—then again, a normal crisis didn't involve the victims of gunshot wounds, but in his life, maybe it did.

"No." She had to agree. Reign took a drink. The wine was truly Italian and delicious, but she was worried about Sal . . . and Nick was infuriatingly right: she couldn't do anything at this point to help him.

Her grandmother had an old saying: "Misfortune comes in by the door left ajar."

*What door is open?* She looked at the man sitting across from her. "What do you think is happening?"

"Unfortunately, someone wants to kill you."

"I can't see how it would benefit anyone." She was genuinely bewildered. Reign set her hands on the plastic placemat that had an exaggerated picture of a plate of spaghetti and took a calm minute to think. "Revenge on my father? Okay, I get it, but he's in prison. Surely that's revenge enough for anyone. Sal was right when he said we shouldn't inherit the sins of our fathers."

"Maybe so, but the trouble with this game is you don't get to write the rules. You want it to be fair. It isn't, sweetheart."

When she pictured Salvatore crumpling to the deck, a bloody hand to his stomach, she didn't really view this as a game. "I'm not—"

"Yes, you are." Nick leaned forward, his elbows on the table. He'd put his tailored jacket back on but still didn't have a shirt, and with her blood-stained dress, they had to make some pretty interesting patrons, even if it was getting late and the place was dark and only one other table was occupied. "You're trying to make sense of it. Quit that. So far this seems to be coming at you blind and we need to figure out why, and more importantly, who.

I promise, you know who it is. No one goes to this much trouble after a casual target. Doesn't happen."

Okay, he had a point, but he also had a disturbing habit of being able to handle volatile situations with this sort of pragmatic approach. It was fine if you were on his side, but she'd hate to be on the other end.

Reign just didn't have an answer. Considering the family feud, she might have said before this that Sal's family would be the first candidate, but they would never have shot *him*.

"I don't know." It was an honest answer.

The arrival of their food stopped the discussion and she was surprisingly hungry, so maybe Nick was right. New York–style pizza, with a thin crust that could be folded and a glass of wine . . . it wasn't like she wanted a lot, but she did manage to eat some, and he'd nailed it in that she felt better afterward. The wine didn't hurt either.

Smart guy.

No, *wise* guy.

Her whole life she'd tried to avoid just this sort of man. Reign looked at him across the table. "You aren't good for me."

Nick looked unfazed. He took another piece of pizza. "You have it entirely wrong. The real question is, are we good *together*?"

"In bed we are."

"I won't argue that one. Not a bad place to start from my point of view."

Reign sighed. "I'm too worried about Sal right now to get into a deep philosophical discussion about male/female relationships and how they work. We've recently met, and it seems like two of the evenings we've spent together have turned out to be pretty interesting, and not in a good way."

"I know. Let me settle this up and we'll go find out how he's doing." He stood, tall in the dim lighting, his face all angles and shadows. "You do realize they probably won't tell you anything. They'll talk to his family, and from what I now understand, his family is unlikely to pass the information on to you."

*He was right, damn him.* Reign murmured, "But maybe to you. How do you know Sal's family well enough to get an invitation to a party on their yacht?"

He dropped enough bills on the table that the waitress was going to be a very happy person. "Through my father. Shall we go?"

Okay, he didn't want to talk about his family. It was there in the clipped tone of his voice. Fine. She got it. There were bits of her past she didn't want to discuss either, especially her ex-husband. Family was family, and keeping it private was important.

"Yes. Thanks."

The least she could say.

"For dinner? My pleasure."

"No, not for dinner." She set her hand on his arm. "For giving a shit about how I feel about this situation. About another guy. You're being very nice."

His blue eyes were hard to read, but he looked at her directly, and she liked that. "I do give a shit, Ms. Reign Supreme. I'm not positive I want to, but

I give a shit. But never, ever make the mistake of thinking I'm nice."

She walked out into the parking lot and looked over her shoulder. "Oh, don't worry. I don't make that sort of mistake."

Machines were beeping, but he expected that, even as he roused from a sleep that was hardly refreshing, the muscles in his stomach tightening as he instinctively tried to sit up.

*Bad idea.*

Right. Shot twice. Sal winced as he relaxed back down and remembered the evening. Shot in front of Reign. Not ideal. There he'd been, trying to be smooth and persuasive, and then out of the blue, two bullets ruined the effect.

"Good morning." The voice was low and modulated, an alto not a soprano, and the person speaking picked up a chart hanging from the foot of the bed and flipped through the pages. Light blue scrubs, brown hair in a ponytail, and honey-colored eyes. She glanced at him. "I'm Dr. Altea. How are you feeling?"

He suddenly wished, even in his incapacitated state, that he wasn't wearing a hospital gown. So maybe he wasn't quite dead yet. "Like someone shot me in the shoulder and the stomach."

"Well then, from your chart, we are on the same page. What a coincidence. Any nausea?"

"Now or when it happened? I don't like the sight of blood much, so when I think back on it, maybe a little."

He adjusted the bed, looked at the attached sacks of fluid and the tubes running into his arm, and briefly closed his eyes. The thing about hospitals was the smell. He could do without it.

The doctor was much more matter-of-fact. She said, "Mr. Ariano, I'm serious. The shoulder injury was clean, but the wound to your abdomen nicked the colon. It was a surprisingly easy repair, but we need to watch you closely and I very much want you to keep me in the loop on how you are feeling. This is not the time to grit your teeth and not complain." She flipped over a page and frowned. "You did have some alcohol in your system, but not much."

"I was standing on the deck of my parents' yacht during a cocktail party. I wasn't driving the boat either. Give me a break. I'd had a drink or two. Not against the law."

"Yes, I recognized the last name." Dr. Altea hung up the chart. "But I was actually about to congratulate you on being so conservative. The surgery would have been a lot more dangerous if you were intoxicated."

"I'll keep that in mind if I ever get shot again."

Finally she cracked a smile, and she was quite

pretty, even if it was in a wholesome way that was
more Midwestern country girl than anything else,
as she moved around the bed and took his pulse. She
took out her stethoscope and listened to his chest.
"Your parents are outside, but I wanted to see you
first and confirm you are up for visitors."

He wasn't sure.

"For the record, a visit with my mother can send
a person to the hospital even if they haven't recently
been shot."

She smiled at his dry tone. "Shall I tell them ten
minutes is the time limit of their stay?"

"God bless you." After a brief hesitation, he said,
"Doctor, is anyone else waiting to see me?"

"Long dark hair? Very striking?"

"Yes." His voice sounded hoarse.

The doctor opened the door to his room but
leaned back in as she was leaving and said with a
conspiratorial air, "She was here most of the night
in the waiting area, and I advised her to go home
because she wasn't going to get to see you. I have
every confidence she'll be back."

Had to be Reign.

He was an idiot, but it made him happy. "When
she returns, please *let* her see me?"

"I'll let the nurses know."

"Thanks."

"No problem."

God, he felt weak, and there were about fifteen
tubes coming out of him, the catheter being the
worst of it. The idea of someone handling his dick
while he was unconscious didn't thrill him, but at

least he was alive. That second bullet had almost done the job.

And he was left wondering why.

He didn't really dabble in the family business. True, he was in law school so he could be useful to his father, uncles, cousins—he'd started out with an accounting degree for just that purpose. It was just that he couldn't see how he'd made an enemy that powerful without his father hearing about it.

It really wasn't a surprise his mother had at some point gone home and changed her clothes from the flowing long dress she'd worn on the boat. Her hair hung in perfect symmetry just at her jawline and was a carefully colored deep auburn shade—not her natural hue. Even her makeup was flawless, and she carried a purse that he was fairly sure had cost thousands of dollars.

In general they got along, but he had no illusions. First of all, he'd ruined her party by getting shot, and secondly, he was pretty sure his relationship with Reign—wait, his *former* relationship with Reign—was now obvious.

This just was not going to be the best conversation of his life, so it was better to take the initiative.

"Do you know why?" He directed the question at his father, who had walked in with a grim expression behind his mother. "Because I'm fairly certain it was not about anything I've done."

"There's nothing on the street." His father shook his head. In his youth he'd also been blond, but his hair had gone to gray; he'd kept himself fairly fit and was a scratch golfer. If there was a connection in New York City or Jersey he had it, and at the moment he didn't look all that forgiving about the incident.

He looked thoroughly tired and pissed off.

"I have people listening. When they hear something, I'll take care of it. You have my word."

From Salvatore Ariano Sr., that was quite a promise.

"I don't really care about revenge." Sal shook his head. "I'm just trying to make sense of it."

"Then you are the only one in this room that doesn't care about revenge."

Sal laughed a little, and it hurt his stomach like being branded with a glowing hot piece of iron. "Okay, but let's just say I'm not so much interested even in who did it as in not having it happen again."

Unthinkable at the moment. He'd never been shot before and didn't wish to repeat the experience. Sal added, "You really have no idea?"

"Honestly, Son, I don't. This blindsided me."

"How well do you know Reign Grazi?" His mother had sat down in the chair next to the bed. She reached over and touched his face, but her fingertips were cold and her expression hard.

"This isn't her fault."

"Salvatore, I don't think that was the question."

"Intimately," he responded because he really wasn't much of a liar anyway, and his mother always knew if he even tried it. Under the hostess persona she was pretty shrewd. "Like if she would consider it, which she won't so don't panic, I'd marry her."

If he wasn't on some pretty heavy painkillers he'd never have said that, but there it was. A machine beeped into the silence following that admission.

"Over my dead body," his father muttered after a moment, his face shuttered.

"I'm kind of thinking her family feels the same way." Sal pushed the button for more morphine. "Lucky me. This Romeo and Juliet bullshit is archaic."

"Don't be a smartass. Maybe Grazi heard about you and his daughter and ordered the hit."

"And risk Reign's life? No way. I happen to know he adores her. Those bullets could just have easily hit her. I want you to do me a favor and find out if, for any reason, there's a contract out on her."

"She was there with Fattelli." His father's voice was crisp and unforgiving.

He'd known all along how they would react, but luckily, it was the least of his problems at the moment.

"Oh, I noticed." Sal was starting to fade a little, zoning out. "That was a lovely moment for me, as you can imagine. The evening only got better. I can't decide if seeing her with him or getting shot was the worst part."

His mother reached over and risked her manicured nails to clasp his hand. "Don't even say that."

With an ironic tone, he said, "Are we now worrying about my possible broken heart, my near-death experience, or how I feel?"

If she answered, he didn't hear it. Thankfully he drifted into la-la land.

Reign listened carefully and heard the prognosis with a lightened sense of what she hadn't realized was such a heavy worry.

The doctor said, "He's stable and we'll move him to a general surgery floor in a few hours. Obviously he lost some blood and that's why he is so out of it. Don't take that as a bad sign. He came through the surgery beautifully, and we are optimistic the rest of his recovery will go the same way."

Several nurses bustled past, one of them pushing a cart, the wheels rattling on the linoleum floor.

"Thank you," Reign said, her voice breaking a little. "No one else will tell me anything."

"He wants to see you."

She wanted to see him too. "How perfect. That's why I'm here."

"I understand you're part of the reason he came through so well." The doctor was young and pretty, wearing scrubs and the usual white coat, her gaze assessing. Absolutely business-like, but the assessment seemed to weigh in some judgment.

She'd done a lot in her life that tested her ability to deal with fellow human beings. Reign lifted her shoulders. "I did my best to stop the bleeding."

"You must have been effective enough, because he is still alive. Are you a nurse?"

"Sal would never bow out without a fight, and no, I'm a fashion designer." She held out her hand. She should actually be at her studio right now because she'd been commissioned to come up with a proposal for a wedding gown for a friend of Giovanna's, but her assistant had keys. "Reign Grazi."

"I wondered." The doctor slid the file in her hand onto the desk and gave Reign a brief shake. "I realize this is New York, and I've heard his family name before, and I've even heard yours . . . but my life would be easier if you all might get along a little better."

"Sal and I," Reign said with a small smile, "get along just fine. Can I go in?"

"Ms. Grazi, I have a feeling he would like nothing better, so please go ahead."

Given permission, she tentatively pushed open the door to Sal's room a few minutes later. He was reclined against the pillow, his face still fairly pale, but he opened his eyes immediately and smiled at her. "Oh. Hi. Wow, you look great."

She did love him. Even with bandages swathed across his bare chest and his hair definitely unruly— not to mention the shadow of a beard—he was good-looking, but that wasn't the reason. That light in his eyes and his boyish smile weren't an act. Sal *was* a nice guy.

Reign knew she had a definite weakness for him. But loving someone and being in love with them— not the same thing.

As the saying went, there was always a "but." Their families hated each other. It wasn't a light enmity either, and it needed to be addressed. He was also younger—enough to give her pause. She wasn't at all sure Vince would be okay with it, though she didn't live her life for him entirely. . . . Her son liked Sal, she knew that. Would he like Nick?

Oh hell, it was complicated, but she needed to see that Sal was really going to be okay.

That was what mattered.

He tried to smile and didn't quite succeed, but it touched her anyway. He said, "I like the dress. Looks good on you."

Form-fitting and dark blue, above the knee, with a hint of white at the lining of the bodice . . . she liked it too. "I designed it."

"I guessed that already."

She crossed over and kissed him. Not on the mouth, but with long lingering pressure on his cheek while she caressed his good shoulder. "How are you doing?"

He felt solid, male, and best of all . . . alive. He said, "Pretty good."

"Let's make a pact to never go through that again. Deal?"

Sal reached across and caught her hand. "Deal. Sit here on the bed with me, not in the chair."

She did as he asked, though his tall body took up most of the space. He interlocked their fingers. "Fattelli out there waiting for you?"

"No. I came alone."

"You shouldn't." He was dead serious. "They could come after you in other ways. Blow up your car, your house. . . . Please tell me you're staying with someone else."

"I'm going to stay with my sister for a few days."

"Why not stay with him?"

"That suggestion from you of all people?" Reign lifted her brows.

"You'd be safer." Sal's fingers tightened. "If this has anything to do with your father, they could go after her too. Or Vince. It's good he's in Long Island right now. Sounds like he's having fun."

That startled her. "You talked to him?"

"After the shooting at your house. He obviously knew nothing about it and I didn't tell him either. I like the kid. I was just checking in."

*Because his father wasn't there for him, you stepped in.* Reign's fingers tightened a little around his also. "That was nice of you. He'll hear about it eventually, but I just don't want to ruin his vacation. It isn't like he's unaware of the Life and certainly knows his grandfather is in jail and why, but I've done my best to give him a fairly normal childhood."

"He's eighteen, Reign. That means no longer a child."

Not new information. She was still adjusting to the idea of her son moving out one day. She'd essentially been a single parent most of his life, so the bond was very close.

She essayed a bright smile. "Yes, I know. He's like you, though, going off to college. It's going to cost me a fortune. Did I tell you I'm being considered for a design position with a firm that handles clothing lines for a major chain? Might be the right time to score that job. I love boutique design and unique pieces, but having my own brand? That's a dream of mine."

His eyes reflected that he completely understood. "How amazing." Then he visibly winced. "I didn't mean it that way. I meant—"

"I know what you meant."

"Make his dad pay half."

She shook her head. "The less we have to do with Ray, the better. I think Vince has learned the hard way to agree with my point of view."

Sal's eyes closed briefly. "I remember that day when I had to make a choice, but I suppose this is the life I know. I took it to the middle of the road. I'm in, but not like Fattelli. He's very old school. From Sicily. You do realize that, right?"

"I am sleeping with him and that's about it."

"Ouch." Sal loosened his grip on her hand.

"You okay?" In alarm, she stood. "Should I call the nurse?"

"No, not the problem."

"Sal,"—her voice held a tone of rueful amusement—"did you think I would suddenly become a nun? He's . . . interesting."

"And very good-looking and Italian. I get it."

"So are you." She smiled again, but she was fairly sure it was strained this time. "It's pretty unlikely he'll fall in love with me, that's the difference. I'm not thinking that's his style."

Sal was getting tired. She could see it in his face, and hell, the man *had* been shot twice. It seemed like everyone, including him, thought that maybe he'd taken those bullets even though they were meant for her.

"You're too guarded," he muttered.

"Only because once, I wasn't guarded enough." She gently pulled her hand from his. "Listen, I think you should get some rest. I'll be back tomorrow. I brought your cell phone." She fished it out of her purse and set it on the table by the bed. "It must have fallen out of your pocket on the boat. Call me if you need anything."

"Stay with Fattelli." He didn't as much as glance at the phone.

She murmured, "I'll think about it, but he actually hasn't asked me. Look, I've got to go to work."

# ELEVEN

How the hell could he convince her?

Nick rubbed his jaw and contemplated his strategy. His apartment had been selected for both the prestigious address and the safety advantages: controlled entry and easy escape possibilities. Reign's house, on the other hand, was on a nice residential street.

Her vulnerability bothered him, and in general he didn't allow that in his life. The upgraded alarm system was going to be helpful, but it was a completely different scenario if a person understood the threat. He knew—no one knew better—that no one could protect himself all the time.

He pushed a button on his phone. Denton's secretary answered and put him right through. "You hear about Ariano?"

The other man said, "Enough to make me leery of the company of Ms. Grazi right now."

"But still no one is talking about it?"

"About it, yes. But if anyone knows anything they are keeping it to themselves. We're all puzzled, Fattelli. First a try at a Grazi, then someone almost takes out an Ariano. Logic tells me maybe the Grazi family blamed the Ariano family for the first hit attempt and retaliated, but my gut tells me that there is a third party involved."

Nick's instincts were in agreement. "You owe me, so keep me posted, okay?"

He hung up and, after a brief hesitation, pushed another button. When she answered, he said abruptly, "Dinner tonight?"

"A 'hello' might be welcome. Not the smoothest invitation ever, Fattelli."

He knew she was at her studio. It wasn't actually that far from where he had his office. He glanced out the window, tapped a key on his computer to send an e-mail, and tried again with exaggerated politeness.

"Ms. Grazi, I think you are the most enchanting creature on this planet, and if you would have dinner with me this evening, I would be honored."

"This isn't 1815, but that *is* better. I'm still at my studio. I've got something to finish up and then I need to go and change. I'm still staying with my sister."

He thought uneasily about her phone, her studio, and her sister's house. "We'll go have a drink or something first. Leave your cell behind, okay? You might want to change purses."

"What? Why?"

"It could have a passenger. I'm wondering how the hell they found you on that yacht. All I said was that I was bringing a date. It's been bothering me."

"A what? Oh fuck, really? Now you sound like Sal. Am I putting Maria in danger?"

"Maybe. But if so, if someone is looking for you, they are already aware of the location."

Silence. Then she asked, "Is there some new information?"

"No. I've just been thinking about it, asking around a little bit." And he had been thinking. All day, staring moodily out the window instead of caring about what was happening on Wall Street. He was doing that now, watching the traffic crawl along, his focus elsewhere.

"What about my son?"

Good question. If he were in her position, he'd wonder about that too. "I don't think he's the target. If this was a revenge deal, they'd have gone after him already."

"That's reassuring," she muttered. "I'm a mother. Unless you have kids, you have no idea how much you're scaring me."

"It's a big bad world out there, but I think it's you they want. Tell him to stay in Long Island for a while. That possible?"

He might have added he knew for certain she was the target, since he'd been approached to take her out.

She said abruptly, "I'll get another phone to call Vince and give him the number."

"Not necessary. I know people. I'll get you a

new phone, and I might carry yours myself for a while, just to see what happens."

"Shit, Nick, don't challenge them."

"Ms. Grazi, I'm interested in *warning* them. Got it?"

There was a slight pause. "I do get it."

"Be ready about six?"

"I was planning on staying late but I can finish what I'm doing tomorrow."

When he ended the call, he checked his Glock, slipped it into his shoulder holster, and put on his tailored dark gray suit jacket. The ingrained habit of always wearing a suit came from his father, along with the legacy of his occupation. He looked professional because he was.

Both occupations.

Forty minutes later, he pulled up to her office building—he got out of the car as Reign came out of the glass doors, his gaze brushing over the street, assessing each vehicle parked there, his hand slipping into his jacket.

Just in case.

But he didn't sense or see anything out of the ordinary—so when she came down the steps, he went around and politely opened the passenger door. "Nice evening for a date."

"Is that what this is? A date?" She slanted him a sardonic glance before she got in. "You know how I like a man with a *weapon*."

He laughed. Reign had a lot of noticeable qualities, but her sense of humor was right up there. "Then you're in luck. I have two."

"Uhm, sounds promising."

She was wearing a strapless sheath in black and really, really had the body for it. Reign caught his appreciative stare as he started the car and lifted her bare shoulders. "I just assumed this would not be a pizza night. I had about two minutes to change. Luckily, I just finished this dress last week and my assistant is a wizard with her sewing machine."

"You assumed right. You look . . . great."

She did, hands down. Those beautiful breasts were displayed in a manner that both tantalized and captured a little too much of his attention. Her cleavage alone might cause an accident. He needed to look away.

*Focus.*

"Thank you."

"Here." He handed her the burner phone and pulled away. "Until we figure all this out. Give me yours."

"Sure."

"Let me call Vince." The set of her mouth spoke even more than the tension in her body. When the brief conversation was over, Reign visibly relaxed. "He's going to stay at the beach house with his friend. The family gets it. . . . We've known them for years."

"Your sister?"

"Decided to visit a friend in the Hamptons." Her smile was ironic. "The timing couldn't be better. I totally encouraged her to go. Maria works too hard anyway. A long walk on the beach and cocktails on the veranda would do her good."

"Smart girl. So you're all on your own?"

"Somewhat."

"Not anymore."

Reign sent him a look. "Oh?"

"We're just getting started. . . . How about you stay at my place?" He negligently shrugged. "For a week or so. Good food, great sex, what's to hate?"

"I hope, Fattelli, you'll be providing the food?" She deliberately stretched out those glorious legs.

"If you provide the sex, sure."

Reign gave a muffled laugh. "I meant that you aren't expecting me to stay with you and wait on you hand and foot."

"Neither my hand or foot are all that interested. My dick, on the other hand—"

"Yes, I kind of guessed that." She sat up a little, her profile suddenly remote. "I truly do not know what is happening. Do you believe me?"

He did. "Absolutely." He didn't know either. That was the problem. Not that she was lying, but she had the key to the lock and just couldn't put her finger on it yet.

"How often does that happen?"

The Bentley rode smoothly around a corner. He'd loved how the car handled from the minute he'd taken it out for a test drive. He took a minute to answer. "How often does a target not have any idea who is coming after them? I don't know. I've never taken a survey."

She said softly, "That wasn't the question. I wanted to know if you *believed* me."

Reign was trusting a man who couldn't be trusted. With her life. It was still surreal to think she'd been a witness to two shootings in such a short span of time, and the sight of Sal in that hospital bed had shaken her to the core. It was all happening too fast, and she didn't really know where to turn. At least Nick was willing to take care of her.

Wait, amend the statement. Was it just the sex?

He'd saved her life once before, so maybe she was being judgmental, and maybe the attraction was part of the problem. . . . But still.

Nick looked fantastic, but he usually did. Gray suit, red tie, dark hair just ruffled a shade more than fashionable, his blue eyes shadowed as he escorted her into the bar. It was dark, but the wall with all the bottles was illuminated, and he settled into a seat with a diffident air she was sure would not last. Then, without asking, he ordered them both Johnnie Black on the rocks.

Okay, big conversation coming.

All her life she'd dealt with alpha males. She knew the signs.

"Let's talk about it and then just have a nice evening," he told her, resting his arm on the polished surface of the bar.

*Yes, big one.* The bartender set a glass down in front of each of them.

"Tell me more about your ex." Nick's gaze was straightforward. "Could all this be him?"

"No. He was a dishonest asshole and I divorced him. End of story." Reign took a drink and gave him back a challenging look. "What about you? Ever been married?"

"No. Back to my question. How bitter was the divorce?"

"If you are suggesting he could be the one who fired those shots . . . I really doubt it. And he's far too cheap to pay someone to kill me. Besides, he doesn't care enough to bother. Trust me on that point. Besides, he'd never risk pissing off the Ariano family."

"You sound sure."

"Because I *am* sure. I know the animal."

"What does your son think about your attitude toward his father?"

"That's a fairly personal question, Nicky. And it isn't an attitude, but an observation."

He quirked a brow. "I think you and I have been fairly up close and personal before, and I'm kind of hoping it will happen again."

She gazed at him. "Like tonight. I'm kind of looking forward to it myself."

"So nice we get along."

So nice he was there, with those wide shoulders and a protective air she found a little surprising but was welcome, if she admitted it. Between him and Sal she was feeling a little bit . . . cherished.

Except for that person who apparently had contracted a hit on her.

Soft music played in the background. Something jazzy, no lyrics, just instrumental. The bar was filling up and she noted that Nick took a look at every single person who entered the place. It was well done and casual, and if she hadn't been sensitive to it she might not even have noticed he was that good, but yes, he was *watching*.

And pretty much every woman that walked in at least glanced at him. Why not? He was handsome and polished and even the way he lifted his drink to his mouth was somehow sensual.

She considered him. "Ever even thought about getting married? Surely you're . . . hmm, I don't even know how old you are."

"Never said." He laughed lightly. "But you didn't ask either."

"If I asked?"

"I might tell you the truth, but only because I'm trying to get you into bed again. It doesn't matter, does it? You would never know unless you were able to get a copy of my birth certificate, now would you?"

"All the way from Sicily?"

"Might be a bit of a problem. How do you know that?"

"Sal told me."

"He has a big mouth. How was he when you visited him?"

Reign remembered his ashen color, but also the strong grip of his hand. "Doing pretty well. He told me to stay with you. He's jealous, but worried about me."

"What a coincidence, I'm jealous but worried about you too." Nick ran his finger along the rim of his glass. The lighting sent shadows along his cheekbones. "All right. I'm thirty-seven going on about a hundred and thirty-seven. I was born in Sicily and my parents brought me here really young. Now it is your turn. Give me something personal about you."

"This *is* like a date."

"Only I'm not just pretending to be interested to get you into bed. I really want to know you."

Reign finished her drink—she noticed he was a bit slower about his—and said provocatively, "You aren't trying to get me into bed?"

"Was I dreaming or didn't you already agree?"

"No, you weren't dreaming." She shook her head. "Get me a refill and I'll do my best to answer the question. I just have no idea what it is you want to know."

He leaned forward. "The woman. I want to know the real woman. The mob wife. The fashion designer, the mother . . . the sexy lady wearing that dress. You've got to admit there's a lot going on there and I'm trying to put it all together."

She was sure he was going to kiss her then and there. His mouth was inches away. The music hummed in the background.

But then he straightened and signaled the bartender. "Think about it for a minute. I want a clever answer. Something you wouldn't just tell anyone."

"Think you're special, Fattelli?" Was she disappointed or just intrigued by his sudden withdrawal? It seemed like he checked himself at the last minute.

"I'm sure trying to be. Let me order you another drink."

Reign watched him move smoothly down the bar, thinking about her answer. When he came back a few seconds later and looked at her expectantly, she said casually, "Maybe when my drink actually arrives. . . ."

"Stop putting me off. Give up one thing."

"I gave up my virtue already." Her reply was dry.

"I appreciated it too. One thing," he coaxed, and he really had the most gorgeous eyes and that killer sexy smile.

Reign decided to compromise. "One small thing since you are so damn curious about me."

"I'll take what I can get."

"I love sushi."

"Hmm. Nice start. Not that surprising, I suppose. Italy is surrounded by water. We are a fish-loving people."

"Your turn again." She accepted another glass from the bartender with a smile of thanks.

"I hate spiders. Creepy-crawly things. No thanks. Go. What's your favorite color?"

"Green."

"Like your eyes? Mine too. That exact exquisite shade."

"Are you trying to flatter me?" The scotch had at least taken the edge off of what had been a stressful day.

"I doubt I need to. You know you are beautiful."

It was time for this conversation to be over. "So where are we going?"

"As it happens I'm taking you out for sushi. I hadn't picked a restaurant yet, so you see, that little tidbit made my life easier."

"Sounds delicious."

"And then back to my place."

She took a sip of scotch. "Very smooth."

"Thank you."

"I was talking about my drink."

He lifted his glass to his mouth and murmured over the rim, "How I love a woman with a smart-ass sense of humor."

# TWELVE

He practically backed Reign through the doorway of his apartment because he was that damn hungry for her. She made the mistake of turning around to ask him something after he stood back to let her go inside first, and Nick caught her around the waist. "The answer is whatever you want it to be. I've been waiting all night to touch you. Have I mentioned you look sexy with chopsticks in your hand?"

She didn't resist and fit against him . . . perfectly. "Are we in some kind of hurry?"

"For the first time, maybe."

Her lashes lowered. "Arrogant, aren't you?"

But she kissed him. He was a little surprised that it was not strictly hot and passionate on her side, when he knew firsthand she was a very sexual woman, but more sweet and almost romantic. A feather brush of her lips first, then greater pressure but still gentle, and he had to do everything in his power not to take over but let her control the pace.

When she broke away, she murmured, "That was a thank you for a nice evening when I would have sworn that to be impossible."

"It's about to get nicer." Nick decided to go theatrical and picked her up so swiftly her purse fell from her hands and hit the floor of the foyer. "I just need a convenient horizontal surface to get the party started."

"You *are* in a hurry."

"Seems that way. I have this vague memory of the most incredible sex of my life and need to refresh it."

"Why do I doubt your memory is ever vague?"

She was all too right. In his position, one slip and he might be dead.

Ignoring the observation seemed best. He carried her into his bedroom and deposited her on the bed. "While I love your dress, let's move on to the good part, agreed?"

"Don't go crazy and I did mention it was just finished, right? It unzips on the side. Let me do it." She slipped the zipper down and Nick watched the sensuous movement of her hand with a satisfying sense that whatever was about to happen, he was going to enjoy it very, very much.

She slid it down and shimmied out of it. "Built-in bra. Much easier, and I know you find underwear to be an annoyance. Besides, I have the advantage of having a lot of my clothes custom made just for me when I do a design."

"How did I know you were naked under that dress?" He had been imagining it all evening and had the hard-on to prove it.

"Good guess?"

It was true. She was nude, having already kicked off her heels.

Nick had to admit his urgency level was pretty high. He ran a finger around her nipple. "I highly approve."

"Of my dress?"

"That too."

"Thought you might."

"Ever think about getting a Brazilian wax?" His gaze was moved lower. "If so, don't do it. I find it an affront to mess with perfection, and though your tits and ass would be quite the attraction on a crowded beach in a thong bikini, I'd rather be the only man looking at your body."

"It's always sounded kind of painful anyway." Reign wiggled backward on the bed. "You got it."

*For how long?*

Nick shed his clothes as swiftly as possible and joined her, pinning her down. He rubbed his cock against the warmth between her legs. "I'm already pretty primed," he admitted. "That damned dress. You did that on purpose."

"Is it a crime to try and look nice?"

No, it wasn't, but it was almost a crime for her to be so attractive. He just wasn't used to losing any measure of control, but . . .

One moment later, with no foreplay except her earlier kiss, he had a condom on and was spreading her legs wider with his knees. "It has to be now," he told her without apology. "I can't wait."

"Then don't." It was an audacious reply matched by the willing position of her body.

His entire life his mother had carefully explained to him that when he met the right woman, he would know it.

No. This was sex, not anything more, and that was just how Reign wanted it. Wasn't it?

Involved. He was too involved.

"I've changed my mind. I want to have your breasts in my hands." He urged her over to her stomach. "New position. Do you mind?"

To her credit, she did go to her hands and knees, all that long black hair spilling over her back. "No."

Even as he entered her, he had to wonder briefly about the man who would walk away from this particular woman. Artistic, gifted with a unique beauty, and that fascinating sense of independence. . . .

Her ex-husband was an idiot.

Of course, Reign was still not perfect, but then again, no one was.

Stubborn. Beyond that. Far too private . . . he'd give on that score, since he was too, and maybe she'd earned it. Intelligent. Sexy. Interesting.

Nick knew he was losing his train of thought. She was tight and hot and he was finally inside her after a long evening of imagining how good it was going to be. Introspection could wait for later. Right now he needed to make love to her.

*Dangerous thinking.* Right now he needed to satisfy them both in a sexual way, keep her safe, and wake up in the morning with her in his arms.

Oh shit. That *was* making love.

Reign arched her spine in response when his hands slid to her breasts and he pushed deep inside her. He kissed the back of her shoulder. "Damn, you feel so tight and hot."

"Dirty talk. Nice. Always spices it up. Keep it up."

Nick laughed and began to move. "I think we're past that. You have a really great firm ass."

"Go faster." It was an order.

"No worries." He held her in place and started to really thrust because it wasn't going to take long.

And it didn't. He lost it quickly, his climax swift and so pleasurable he had to prevent himself from collapsing on top of her but stayed on his knees, letting it happen and then begin to fade.

When he slipped out of her lissome body and dropped down on the bed, he muttered, "I think I owe you for that one. Ask for whatever you want."

"I think you'll come up with something." Her hand swept his chest, and Reign rolled on top of him, her mouth warm as she kissed him. "Just make it good."

It was good already having her naked and willing in his arms. That would motivate any man.

"You have doubts?" His voice was amused, but that had been a fairly fast race to the finish and he held her loosely against him.

"I have doubts about every single man I meet."

Was she serious? It gave him pause. "Reign."

"No. You have to prove yourself to me."

It certainly sounded like she meant it.

"I suppose to a certain extent I feel the same way," he admitted, reaching up to touch her face. "Trust is a hard-earned commodity. You and I are alike in a lot of ways. We were both born into a certain kind of lifestyle. This life was chosen for us in my opinion, without our specific consent."

Reign's eyes held a reflective look. "I love my family. I'd do anything for them. The same for my close friends."

"Salvatore Ariano included?"

"Do you really want to talk about another man right now while we're in bed together?" She reached down and gently squeezed his thigh, then moved her hand to his cock. Her fingers circled and exerted a little pressure. "Let me see if I can get you interested again because I'm feeling a little left out right now."

Nick said in a thick voice, "You won't be for long if you keep doing that."

It was flattering she could make a man like Nick lose control. Reign doubted it happened very often, and his attraction to her seemed both genuine and intense. She lay back against the pillows and savored the stroke of his hands over her shoulders and breasts, as they moved down her torso to her hips and thighs. The touch was erotically delicate and very arousing.

"This one is for you, but I hope you don't mind if I enjoy it too," he murmured against her nipple before he took it into his mouth and began to suckle. The swirl of his tongue sent nice tingles of pleasure through her whole body.

"Please do," she managed to say, threading her fingers through his hair.

"Such a generous woman." He moved his mouth to the other breast, taking time to lick the valley between them.

The sensation was enough to make her give a low moan, and Nick raised his head to smile for a moment. "You like that. Continue?"

"Stop and you'll really regret it, Fattelli."

"How come it is that every time you use my last name, I feel like I'm being threatened?"

"Are you afraid of me?" Reign playfully rubbed the back of his calf with her foot.

"Oh yeah," he said softly, holding her gaze before he lowered his dark head again to her breast as his fingers slipped into her pussy.

The dual sensation was nice but not as good as having him inside her.

*Wait for it. . . .*

At that last crucial moment, she ordered, "Now."

He rose above her and ripped open another foil packet with his teeth. "I thought you'd never ask."

"Then we really do need to get to know each other better, Nicky."

"My intention," he said silkily as he entered her, his muscular arms braced on either side of her body.

It was her turn to lose it quickly, but then again,

he'd done a good job of making sure she was ready for it.

They were starting to get to know each other's bodies. He knew just the right angle, and he wasn't shy without actually being rough in any way. He moved and she moved with him, and at the end of it they were both panting and apparently speechless, because the room was quiet except for a vague echo of the traffic on the street far below.

Reign's hand clasped his taut buttock. "Hmm. Let's do that again sometime."

"I'm kind of thinking we will."

The weight of his body was pleasant and she was in a good place, satisfied and tired. Dinner had been at a trendy place that made it hard to carry on a conversation but had excellent food, and she really hadn't eaten much lately. No prices on the menu, and the seafood had been so fresh she was sure it had been incredibly expensive, but he hadn't blinked an eye.

Paid with cash always, she noticed.

But he would. Cautious man.

Nick smoothed her hair. "Can I tell you a story?"

"Hmm. Bedtime story? That's an interesting line I haven't heard yet."

He was still in the cradle of her thighs, but his face had taken on a curiously unreadable expression. "Once upon a time, there was a gorgeous Italian girl with an unusual name."

When she opened her mouth to say something, he stopped her with fingertips to her lips. "No comments please. I'm telling the story."

"Fine." Reign was amused in a languid way. That had been quite an orgasm. "But this seems like an interesting position for this story."

"I like it right where I am." He nibbled on her earlobe. "Can I go on?"

There was something in his voice that suddenly made her wonder if she really wanted to hear it, but she agreed. "Go on."

"One day a very bad man asked another man if he might be willing to take money for killing the pretty Italian lady. He recognized her family name, but didn't know much about her, so he hesitated. This might sound odd, but he has a certain code, and unless he agrees the target deserves it, he won't take the job."

"This isn't exactly a bedtime story." Reign tensed. "Get off me."

Nick didn't budge. "Relax. Listen. I'm trying to explain something to you."

"Is that why we met? Because you were hired to *kill* me?" Shoving at his shoulders was like trying to move a solid brick wall. He wouldn't give an inch.

"I just pointed out I said no thanks."

"Is there a reason I should believe you? Damn you, I hate liars." Her eyes filled with unwanted tears and she blinked them back. Sal had called her guarded. She was, but not guarded enough apparently. It was galling to realize her defenses weren't as solid as she thought they were.

Nick emphatically shook his head. "Reign, stop it. I haven't lied to you one time. I'm sure you get that the end of the story is that the man decided to protect her instead. A new role for him, but he's pretty into it."

There was no question she'd be foolish to buy into the sincerity in his eyes, but then again, she should have listened to her instincts before and right now the vibe was positive. With Ray she'd never really trusted him, and it had been just a feeling. She whispered, "Don't lie to me. Please."

"Once again, I never have. In fact, I was just very honest with you." Nick slowly withdrew and rolled to his back, naked and very male but she wasn't intimidated for some reason; maybe the thoughtful frown between his brows. "I can't figure this situation out. You can't either, and you are an intelligent woman. Please see it from my side."

It was possible no two people ever needed to talk about anything more.

Tightly, she said, "Fine. We need to talk about it. I can't believe you ever—"

"I didn't know you. From the very beginning I wondered why the hell anyone would want to take you out. It makes no sense. That's why when Joey Carre got me an invitation to the party, I accepted. I wanted to meet you."

The ripple of muscle as he turned on his side was impressive, and she was reminded again of how vulnerable she was, which was actually reassuring in a convoluted way. If he had wanted to hurt her, he'd had enough opportunities and certainly the strength to do it.

Okay, maybe he meant it.

*Fuck,* she trusted him.

In an unsteady voice, she told him, "If you ever, ever betray me—"

"I'm not going to do that. We've established it." He stroked her bare hip. "Reign, let's face it, I've had a lot of chances. I have one now. I'm interested in the hit on an intellectual basis, not a monetary one. So talk to me. Let's really try to figure out why. I'm telling you, there's an answer, we just can't see it yet."

T hat didn't go well.

*Damn.* The voice inside his head had told Nick he should just keep his mouth shut.

But his heart said unless he was honest with her, she'd never quite understand how much danger she was in, and Reign was not someone who worried about herself first.

Look at the situation: Her son, safely away on Long Island. Her sister, on her way to the Hamptons.

Look at her. In *his* bed.

"Do not go all Italian on me," he said as calmly as possible as she sat up in a flurry of shining dark hair. "I'm very much interested in figuring this out. No one takes a hit out on someone else without some sort of profit on the other end. It's business or revenge. There are no other motives. So please tamp down that impulse you have to do me bodily damage and accept that I'm not going to hurt you, but someone else wants to do so."

"That's why you weren't at all concerned over Vince."

She looked more beautiful than ever with fire in her green eyes.

"I knew firsthand it was you they were after, yes. Aren't you relieved? One is already dead, and *I'm* not going to do it, so relax."

"I ought to cut your balls off."

"I *could* have never told you."

"You waited long enough."

"Reign, we are on the same side, right? Besides, I don't think your current ensemble of entirely naked could effectively hide a knife."

That seemed to stop her, though she looked pretty delicious on her knees next to him, bare breasts quivering with each outraged breath. At any moment he could tumble her back over, but he respected her anger and the process it took for her to absorb the information.

To her credit, after a moment, she said quietly, "I get your point."

"Let's do this. You take my robe, and I'll get us some wine, and we can sit on the terrace overlooking the city and talk about it. I'm paying a lot of money for this place, so we should at least enjoy the view."

"Where did you get all this money? You have this place and that fabulous car . . . blood money?"

"If you want the truth," he said mildly. "It isn't what you think. I really am fairly good at the stock

market. Learned it early on and invested wisely."
Nick walked, naked, to the closet, aware of her
watching him. He took out a silk robe and turned
to offer it. "Does rich turn you off? If it does, you
are not like any other woman I've met."

Reign was . . . well, Reign. She got up off the
bed and took his robe, wrapping it around her. She
looked him in the eye. "I'm not against rich, and
I'm not for it either. The man impresses me, not his
money."

"How am I doing so far?"

"I'm still wavering on how to answer that."

He picked up his discarded pants. "I'll open that
wine since we seem to be in a semi-truce. Okay?"

"Nothing sweet."

"Wouldn't dream of it. Do you have a preference?"

"Merlot."

"Done."

She did cooperate to the extent that she went and
chose a chair and stared out at the lights of the skyscrapers. The evening air cool against his bare chest,
Nick joined her, bringing two crystal glasses and the
open bottle. He set it all on the glass table between
them. "I suppose you want to know now who tried
to hire me."

It would be *his* first question.

"That would be helpful." Reign shot him a swift,
resentful look. Forgiveness was not anywhere near
happening yet. The sin of omission was definitely
not overlooked.

"The man I shot in your closet. I recognized him

the minute I pulled open that door to make sure he was actually out of the game."

It didn't surprise him she looked confused. "What? That makes no sense. If he was willing to do it himself, why try to hire someone else?"

Nick took a sip of wine and stared out over the lights of the city. The view really *was* worth the exorbitant amount he paid in rent. "I know. I started to have a few doubts at that point. I wish I hadn't killed him, but really, I was just returning fire. He and I would have had an interesting conversation before an ambulance was called. Why the hell was he there?"

"I've already said—"

He interrupted. "I remember. You have no idea who could be doing this. That's what I don't like. If you bump up against an enemy and understand the underlying vendetta, I can deal with that. This is strange. I want to fight back for you, but I am not sure what direction to turn. Do you have an objection to me visiting your father?"

She contemplated a moment, but then said in a small voice, "I guess not. Maybe he needs to get involved in this. He knows everyone."

"Do I sense a glimmer of trust?"

"Did I say I wasn't going with you?"

That actually would be better. He doubted her father would open up to a stranger without her assurance the questions were legitimate. "That'll make an interesting date."

"If you think I haven't visited my share of prisons, think again. I doubt you're a stranger either."

"No comment."

She leaned back and regarded him with a hint of accusation still in her gaze. "You sure don't talk much about your past, do you? I feel kind of naked. Here you seem to know everything about me, and I know very little about you except you were born in Sicily and have an aptitude for sex and money."

"Was that a compliment? I think it was. Besides, I really like you naked."

She crossed her ankles. "And a criticism too."

"I noticed that." The brilliant skyline was accentuated by a crescent moon that hung above the city. Nick knew she needed something back. "I meant the naked part."

"This is entirely the wrong time to be funny, Fattelli."

"Fine." He took in a breath and thought about Carl Denton. "I've called in a few favors myself. There's no noise on the street. I've had a hard time believing it, but nothing."

"But they tried to hire you and apparently two others who took it on."

"It looks that way."

"Looks?" She made a derisive noise.

"This is a discussion, not an explanation. I really don't have anything to explain."

"Like hell. As much as I'm in this, so are you."

That struck him.

She just could be right.

*Oh fuck.*

He drank the rest of his wine and set down the

glass with a definite click. "Have I ever mentioned I think you are as smart as you are beautiful?"

This was . . . stupid.

Dr. Jennifer Altea thought that rarely applied to her, but apparently, she was wrong.

First example: she'd picked out a sundress she hadn't worn since undergrad—thankfully, she still fit into it—and matching shoes, and though her white coat balanced the ensemble with a professional touch, it was still pretty clear she was dressing as a woman and not a doctor.

Oh, she could use the excuse that she was just on call and brush it off that way, but actually no one had called her. She looked at the nurse in charge of the desk and said, "I have a date this evening so I'm doing rounds early."

*Lie.* She was doing rounds early, but there was no date unless a person could count dinner with her older sister as a date.

"And how is Mr. Ariano?" She asked it casually enough.

"Cute." Stephanie grinned. "Like really, really cute. And polite too. Nice combination."

Like she hadn't noticed.

Jennifer leveled what was supposed to be a look of reproof at her. "I was referring to his medical condition. Anything I need to know?"

"No." The nurse shrugged. "He's recovering well and has no complaints. He wanted the catheter out in the worst way, but he's ambulatory now, so we did it."

She didn't *think* he would complain, despite her warning he should be candid, but she had wondered. As a physician it worried her. "No fever?"

"No. If you look over the chart, he's doing excellent."

It did appear everything was normal, from lab tests to wound care.

"Great." Jennifer smiled and headed toward his room. Just another day at the hospital, being the attending physician, but at the moment, it was possible she was just acting like a woman.

Yeah, well, there was a reason for that.

Salvatore Ariano had his hospital gown on with the front open, probably because it was easier to let the nurses check his dressings, which meant there was a nice expanse of muscular bare chest visible. He really wasn't watching the television perched in the corner of the room, but it was on and the screen flickered, and he stared at it moodily as she entered until he registered her presence.

It was unprofessional to be attracted to a patient.

But she was. He looked gorgeously masculine with his tousled blond hair and sculpted features, but he was . . . once again, a patient.

His first words were succinct once he saw her. "Can you just release me?"

"Hello to you too." She flipped through his chart. "Blood pressure is good and there is no sign of infection. I believe that we can release you soon."

He exhaled raggedly in obvious relief. "Thank

God. I'm so close to finishing school, and I've put a lot into this. I don't think what I've missed will make or break me since all we are doing right now is getting ready for the bar exam, but every minute counts."

"I remember studying for my boards."

"Then maybe you understand my current state of mind."

Jennifer hung the chart on the peg at the foot of the bed. "Sure do. But keep in mind if you overtax your body, which has recently had more than a little stress, you are not going to do well no matter how much you study. I'm going to check your vitals, look at your injuries, and then you and I can talk about when you might be released. Good with you?"

"Whatever you say, Doc."

When he genuinely smiled, she felt an odd flutter in the pit of her stomach. It almost irritated her. *Why, of all people, this man?*

Fine, he was good-looking. So? She saw good-looking professional men every single day. He had ties to a lifestyle she knew existed, but didn't quite understand, and those ties were undoubtedly why he was currently in her care.

He'd been shot, for God's sake.

Not to mention the dark-haired woman with the body to die for that he had been so anxious to see. Jennifer had watched her walk past the desk and at that moment understood the level of competition was set pretty high.

Bending over, she took the stethoscope and

looped it automatically into her ears. His heart sounded steady and strong, and next she lifted his wrist to check his pulse. He smelled clean and male and she did her best to ignore it.

*Medicine 101. Do not be attracted to a patient.*

But she was.

Like *really* was.

Jennifer stepped back, looping her stethoscope back around her neck. "Everything sounds good and looks good. I see no reason to keep you if you feel like you can manage the situation on your own. I could release you tomorrow."

"Where are you going tonight?" His gaze lowered to take in her bare legs. "Looks like this is your last stop before a hot date."

Oh hell, he'd picked up on the vibe. Well, she'd wanted him to, but . . .

"I don't really do hot dates." She wrote down the vitals in this chart.

"Uhm." Salvatore Ariano looked amused. "That's a pity. I can tell you they are more fun than the other kind. They are to hell and gone better than lying in a hospital bed. So, no hot date? What do you do for fun?"

It struck her that no one had asked her that question . . . ever?

Really?

She worked too hard. That she knew. Her life was grueling hours and on-call weekends, and while she got hit on with annoying frequency, no one had really asked her that before. To her embarrassment, she admitted, "I think I might have forgotten about fun."

"Classic overworked doctor?" He lifted dark blond brows. "That story has been told too many times. You have to come up with a new one."

"There's a reason it has been told."

"Maybe so," he said softly. "You look really great."

She was pretty enough but not a knockout, and she rarely bothered with makeup or her hair. Maybe she should more often. "Thank you."

"Just a sincere observation."

Was he flirting? She didn't really think so, but at least he was paying attention. Well, kind of. His eyes drifted shut.

The first thing she'd prescribe was rest, so that worked out just right.

When she walked back to the nurses' station, she said, "He's asleep."

"He *was* shot twice."

"I'm aware." She jotted down a few notes. "Let's try this and if he feels he can leave, we'll let him go tomorrow."

The nurse took the file. "Okay, you've got it."

"But he needs to schedule an appointment with my office."

"Yes, Doctor."

"Mind telling me why you are laughing, Steph?"

The nurse leaned forward with a conspiratorial air. "Because I think you might just have a crush on gorgeous Mr. Ariano. Relax, it happens."

# FOURTEEN

The phone call came at exactly nine o'clock. Reign looked at the caller ID absently and then registered the number.

Yes, a part of her went cold, then hot, and then cold again. . . .

"Hello."

"Ms. Grazi?"

Sitting at her desk in her office, she nodded because her throat was dry, but then realized the person on the other end of the call couldn't see her and said, "Yes."

"I think I have some news you will be happy to hear."

Already her heart was racing. *Calm down.* "Needless to say, good news is always welcome. I recognize the number, Mr. Gregory."

"One of our largest clients has decided they very much like your style and they want you to premiere a new line of clothing for sophisticated young women. I can't tell you how many talented designers vied for this contract, so feel free to be very flattered. You've earned it."

It had not been the easiest past few days, so she dipped her head and took a deep breath before she said, "This *is* wonderful news."

"It sure should be. Do you want the numbers of what they are offering?"

She did. They were staggering.

"That much?" Her voice actually was off-key.

"Oh yes. And if the line does well, a lot more. You'll have to travel some when they launch the new lines for each season, but I am sure you anticipated that would be the case."

*A lot more if it was a success.* That would be helpful with Vince about to depart for college. They'd already come to an agreement that he would live near campus on his own rather than make the commute, and that alone was going to be extravagant.

Reign slipped into her professional mode. "Thank you so very much for this opportunity and the phone call. Please tell them that this will be my first priority, and have someone send the ideas for the line and the dates when they want the designs delivered."

"Very good. Congratulations, Ms. Grazi."

*Yes.*

Immediately she called her sister on her cell. "Guess what."

Maria said, "A conversation that begins like that can go one of two ways, and from recent events, I am a little worried about what you are going to say next. Make it simple for me, please. I'm having a Bloody Mary while sitting in a deck chair on the beach."

However it had come about, Maria needed a vacation, so Reign was glad to hear she was making at least an attempt to relax.

She picked up a pen and drew a happy face on an invoice sitting on her desk. "I got the design job."

Maria was silent for maybe a full minute.

"You still there?" Reign was flying high and a laugh bubbled from her throat. "Like . . . got it. They chose me. . . . *Me*."

Then Maria said, "OMG. Are you serious? Don't get me wrong, I never thought you couldn't do it, I just figured it was a long shot at best. . . . Are you *kidding*?"

"I'm not."

"So I think I know who is buying dinner the next time we go out. My treat. Confetti and champagne for everyone. Reign Grazi is on fire."

Well, not completely. Maria had certainly been there for her all her life. "I'm buying for you, for sure." Reign couldn't quite keep the elation from her voice, but she glanced at the quirky clock on the wall. The hands were made from flattened spoons, but it had its own kind of charm, and her assistant had actually made it, so she'd hung it up, and truthfully, it fit the general chaos of material samples, scattered drawings, and paperwork. She needed to get going. "I had to tell you, but I'm going to go pick up Sal. They're releasing him today. He called and asked if I'd come get him. He said he was worried if his mother and father came, they'd insist he come stay with them and he really just wants to go back to his apartment."

"He's okay then."

"Apparently he's recovering really well."

"Apparently so. I'm glad."

"I think we're going to see Dad after that."

"You and Sal?" Maria sounded dubious. "I don't think he needs to leave the hospital and go straight to a prison, Reign. Besides, Dad is not going to want to see an Ariano, we both know that."

"Not Sal. Nick and I."

"Reign, you seem to be getting involved awfully fast and—"

"Save it. I couldn't agree more. I don't know enough about him." She cut her off her sister's protest. "But I like him. He asked to see Dad, and I said yes. We have a few questions."

"Like what?"

Reign could picture her, curling a long piece of dark hair around her finger. Maria tended to do that when she was agitated. *How to do this . . .*

"There have been a few incidents and Nick has wondered if they might be repercussions from the family's past. I don't know either way, and when he suggested our father as a source of information, I thought that might not be a bad way to go."

"Do you know something I don't?" Her sister's voice was heavy with suspicion.

"Actually, no." Reign consciously softened her

tone. "Nick is going to help me. I'm doing this to protect you and Vince."

"Vince needs you to protect him, I don't."

Reign took in a breath. "When will we all wake up and realize we all need each other? I could go wide and suggest that all of mankind figure that one out, but at this point, I am just going to say you and I might need each other and nothing will stop me from protecting my son. How does that sit?"

"Don't be a bitch." There was a hint of laughter in her sister's voice, though it was low-key.

"Yeah, well, don't make me be one."

"Do me a favor?"

*Oh perfect*. Reign said, "Like?"

"Can you tell Dad I said hi?"

Considering the purpose of their visit, it was just as well Maria wasn't able to join them.

"Of course." Reign's shoulders relaxed. "Mar, please."

"It's been a month since I've been there. I've let life get out of hand. Tell him I'll see him next week."

"I will."

After she hung up, Reign called Nick. She'd never done it before and it felt a little strange, but then again, to each thing a season.

"Hello, beautiful." His voice was smooth and mellow and deep.

"Right back at you." Reign kept it light. "I'm heading to the hospital because they are releasing Sal today. How about when he's settled in, we'll go on our visit, and later, out to dinner? My treat."

"I never let a lady pay."

"Then I'll invite someone else." Her voice was silky smooth. "My invitation, my party."

"Maybe I can make an exception just this once."

"For me? I'm flattered."

"What are you in the mood for?"

"Are we still talking food here?"

Reign had to laugh. "Yes, still talking restaurants."

"We'll discuss when I pick you up, okay?"

Almost . . . almost, she insisted she would drive, but he did have a very beautiful car and she could leave her vehicle at Sal's complex, and besides, independent was fine, but militant was unnecessary, in her opinion. She said, "I'll call with the address."

Sal sat on the edge of the bed.

The nurse had given him a bunch of instructions that he duly noted and signed the papers that verified he'd been told, but he was pretty grateful when Reign came into the room. "Here," he said, "if you don't mind, read this over and remind me once we are out of here what I'm supposed to do. I'm crawling up the walls. The doctor just has to come in and sign me out."

She took the papers and her eyes were amused. "I thought paperwork was your thing, Counselor."

"Don't laugh at me. I'm still pretty sore." Luckily he'd remembered to ask his mother to bring him some clothes that were not covered in blood before her visit the day before, and he was about the same size as his father. Currently it looked like he belonged to a very prestigious country club from the insignia on the shirt he wore, and though he would never have chosen the khaki slacks himself, it was still better than his other option.

"I'm sorry." Reign brushed back her hair in a movement he recognized. Her green eyes did hold regret. "There's a part of me that wonders if somehow this isn't my fault, but I don't see *how*."

Today there was no form-fitting blue dress, but she wore a lacy blouse of some kind over a camisole and white skirt, and the contrast to her dark coloring was striking, but she always seemed to be able to pull that off, which just might be why she was in fashion. A career very important to her. He was starting to realize—in his heart of hearts—that what he wanted was not what she wanted. It was painful, but sometimes staring at the truth was better than pushing it aside.

The phrase "love hurts" wasn't exactly comforting, but it had been coined by a realist somewhere apparently.

"Mr. Ariano. Good morning."

Sal tore his gaze from Reign's poignant expression and tried to be at least a little smooth when the doctor walked into the room. "Dr. Altea, thank God. They have actually promised I'm getting out of this joint."

Today she was back to the scrubs and no-nonsense ponytail, which was a far cry from the last time he'd seen her, but she had a wholesome beauty he found attractive.

"Interesting choice of words."

She didn't like his ties to organized crime. Fine. He hadn't asked for her approval. But she did have a nice body. A little on the tall side maybe, but firm and athletic and her hair held an unusual sheen of gold with the brown.

"I'm going to write you a conservative prescription for pain medication." She sat down with a clipboard in a bedside chair. "I want to see you in a week for a follow-up so the wounds can be supervised and cleaned, and unless you have other concerns, I believe I will sign this release."

"What about sex?"

"Excuse me?" Dr. Altea looked startled.

Sal had to admit his head also swiveled on that one, since he wasn't the one who'd spoken.

Reign, still holding the papers he'd handed her, just looked bland. "I meant . . . can he?"

"I suppose so, if he feels up to it." Dr. Altea clicked her pen and set it aside. "There's nothing wrong with that part of his anatomy, but he might still be a bit weak. Just don't get too carried away."

"Oh, I didn't mean me and him. . . . Is that proper English? I think it is. I meant him and you. Now that just doesn't sound right either. Pronouns are annoying." Reign waved a hand. "It doesn't matter, I suppose. Are you interested? It kind of seems to me like you are, and while I was waiting, one of the nurses got a little gossipy. She seemed to think you'd be pleased to know Sal and I are just friends."

The two women eyed each other and suddenly—it was like an out-of-body experience—Sal felt like he was not in the room.

He muttered in protest and nudged her. "Reign, what are you doing?"

They ignored him, still looking at each other.

"I don't know. Is he a good lover?" Dr. Altea—he didn't even know her first name—smiled with a hint of challenge, apparently picking up the gauntlet.

"Oh yeah." Reign smiled back, her green eyes narrowed. "Very good."

That he was currently speechless in this conversation didn't escape him, but he really couldn't think of a single thing to say.

He'd just strangle Reign in the car on the way home.

"Scale of one to ten?" The doctor raised her brows. They were nice too. He didn't like them plucked down to a line, but untidy wasn't his thing either. Hers were just right: finely arched but visible.

"Really up there, and I'm a pretty tough judge." Reign was never one to let something go. "I don't need to ask if you are interested, since I already know you are. Take him out for a test drive sometime."

"For some reason, I thought you two might be involved."

"Were. *Were* involved. So I can speak with some authority on the subject."

It cut, but then again, he'd known in myriad ways it was over. That, and for her general safety, was why he'd advised that she stay with Fattelli. He tried again, "Can I interject something here?"

They answered in sync. "No."

The doctor asked, "He put the lid down?"

Reign said with a slight hint of sardonic amusement, "Not reliably, but he always flushes and washes his hands, and truthfully, he doesn't snore."

"That's huge right there." Dr. Altea laughed. "I'm considering it."

Reign's voice changed tone. Quietly, she said one of the most bittersweet things he'd ever heard in his life. "Sal is a true nice guy. Thoughtful, sweet, handsome . . . he's every girl's dream—but we all look for our perfect fit, and sometimes it isn't that perfection we dream of."

"Very eloquent, Ms. Grazi." The doctor gave Sal a brief glance that he fully returned. "In the meantime," she added in measured tones, "he needs to rest and not overly exert himself and take the wound-care instructions seriously."

"He takes everything seriously." Reign got up and slipped her purse under her arm. "I'm going to wait outside while you wrap this up. I assume he's leaving by wheelchair, so I'll bring the car around. This might be time for the two of you to decide what happens next."

There was, beyond a doubt, a somewhat awkward silence once Reign left. Sal finally said, "She has a slightly unique personality."

"Slightly?" Dr. Altea added on a dark murmur, "And the nurses around here have big mouths."

He lifted his shoulders. "I don't even know what kind of comment to make, so maybe we should just let it go."

"Or talk about it." Dr. Altea took in a breath. "I honestly can't think of a less likely couple than a third-year resident in a prestigious program at one of the best hospitals in the country and a lawyer that I am fairly sure is going to use his skills to help out his family with organized-crime charges. It's ridiculous. It takes it to a new level. I'm from Minnesota."

Sal burst into laughter and it hurt. He clutched his side. "Minnesota? What does that have to do with anything?"

Her lips were pink with only a hint of gloss and very tempting. She laughed with him. "I'm not sure, but St. Paul is not New York City."

"Like that is new information."

She sobered and sighed. "I do think you are an attractive, nice guy. The mob tie sets me back, and my schedule is so crazy it turns off almost every single man I meet. I don't know if I can do anything besides sign off on your release papers and pretend I never met you."

"Or just have dinner with me."

"You are hardly up for a night out. Clear liquids and—"

"I couldn't agree more. In the future?" He was tired and hardly dinner-partner material, but things were looking up. Maybe not with Reign, but he knew some time ago that ship had sailed.

"Maybe."

Not a "no," anyway.

Her eyes were such a lovely shade of topaz. "I'm looking forward to it," he told her.

"I'll write my cell number on your release orders. Call me when you feel up to it, but not before, got it?" She stood.

He said, "I got it."

# FIFTEEN

I t was jarring with the clanging doors, guards, and institutional paint. . . . Reign hated it. She liked to make the world beautiful. Her house was decorated in rich tones: reds and browns and deep blues, and a touch of amber here and there. This would drive her over the edge.

Her father looked maybe a little older each time, but just as handsome as ever and his smile was the one Reign remembered from childhood, warm and charismatic. They faced each other through the glass and she picked up the phone. "Hi."

Very father-like, the first thing he said was, "Who's your friend, sweetheart?"

Was it parental concern or perhaps self-preservation? She couldn't be sure.

"Nick Fattelli." She said it succinctly. "He says you've never met."

"True. But I think I've heard that name before."

"He's got a few questions, and by the way, before

I forget, Maria says hi. She's coming to see you next week."

Reign adored her father. For whatever his faults—and every single person had them—he was genuinely a caring man. "I've missed her," he said, his voice a wisp. "Where's Vince?"

"Out of harm's way. On Long Island with friends. Talk to Nick."

She moved aside, relinquishing the phone. Nick gave her a sidelong look and then took it, settling in the seat. "Mr. Grazi. It's an honor."

"I do know your name. Chicago, right?"

Nick nodded. "I thought you might recognize it. I'm taking good care of her, but . . . we have an interesting situation. On two different occasions there have been shootings in her vicinity and I can't tell you that she wasn't supposed to be the target. If you have thoughts, I'd love to hear any or all of them."

Swiftly, Nick related how he'd been approached, and then he described both shootings in an oblique way that only implied what was going on, but her father got it fast enough.

He frowned. "I have enemies, but I also have friends. I can't see how striking back at me through my little girl would gain anyone anything but a load of trouble."

"What about her ex-husband? She says no."

"I agree. If Ray was going to swing that way, he would have done something years ago, and besides, he knows better. He'd never be seen again. We've had that conversation and I promise you, he knows I mean it."

It was Nick's turn to rub his jaw. "I was kind of hoping you could point me in the right direction."

"Oh, I'll ask the people who would know, believe me."

Nick said evenly, "She's staying with me for now."

"I appreciate it." Her father's voice was grim. "Take good care of her."

"No problem, sir. I've been doing my best."

Nick got up and handed her the phone again. Reign sat back down and said, "I got the design offer I wanted. My own line with my name on it for a prestigious retailer."

"Baby, congratulations."

"Thanks. . . . I'm pretty happy."

"Yeah, well stay happy. Let Fattelli handle this situation, agreed?"

It was hard not to be surprised. Her father was shrewd about people. In fact, he'd told her many times that it was fine to like a stranger, but you were a fool to ever trust one. "I'm pretty self-sufficient," she said slowly. "Always have been, remember?"

"That only works if you know the enemy." Her father's knuckles were white, he was holding the receiver so tightly. "Listen to me. I've heard about him. He's good at what he does, but . . . there's a code, right? That means something right there. That he bothered to come see me is impressive, and that you let him means even more to me. We all make mistakes, but you are a smart girl and always have been. What have I always told you? Use your gut. If he seems on the level, then his particular talents are to your advantage."

Her thoughts exactly, though it had taken her considerably longer to come to that conclusion than this short conversation.

"I'll take that advice under consideration." She gently placed the receiver back in the cradle. Every single time she left she felt like crying and this time was no different. She lifted her chin and fought the emotion.

The fences, the towers . . . God. She couldn't wait to get away, and somehow that felt traitorous.

Reign glanced over at Nick in the car as they pulled away. "So?"

"So?" His expression was neutral. "I thought you were taking me out to dinner. I believe you insisted."

He didn't want to talk about it. Fine, she really didn't either.

He did look very nice in a crisp white shirt and tailored slacks, and she'd chosen something crimson and slinky. "Le Château. We have reservations."

"Sounds fabulous. How many strings did you have to pull for that one?"

"A few. I hope you like French food."

"If I'm having dinner with you, a fast food hamburger would be fine. Why didn't you tell me?"

Reign had to admit she didn't really expect the question. "Tell you? About what?"

"The clothing-line deal." His gaze was focused on the traffic, but she got the impression he was very much paying attention to her reaction. He was affronted on some level too. Hurt? It was hard to tell. Was it even possible to hurt a man like him?

Nick was like that. She'd already figured out that what you saw was not what you got.

And Sal had called *her* guarded?

"I was going to tell you over a glass of fine French wine and an appetizer that probably included escargot or Brie or something."

His wide shoulders relaxed a fraction.

"But," she said quietly, "I don't see my father that often and he has always encouraged me in my career. I told Maria first. She's not just my sister but my best friend. Then I needed to tell him next. He worries about us."

"And he's inside, so he can't take care of you."

"Something like that, I suppose."

"I get it." His expression said he did.

"Did your father ever do time?" She had to admit she was curious about his family. It had started to get dark, the sky deepening to purple above the city.

"No."

This was Nick. He said nothing else, which didn't surprise her. The masculine symmetry of his features was highlighted by the growing dusk and streetlights. His wavy hair brushed his collar.

It was the first—very startling—moment that Reign realized she might fall in love with him.

That wasn't her. She didn't fall in love. Sal didn't count. Who wouldn't fall in love with an idealistic man who was not only beautiful outside but also beautiful inside? Had she realized before their affair started that he was going to be so involved, she never would have allowed it.

It wasn't like Ray either. It had taken a while to admit it to herself, but his easy charm was superficial. He'd wanted to get her into bed, and he'd wanted to have a connection to her family. She'd just been too young and inexperienced to realize her ex-husband was shallow and self-centered, and just because someone said they loved you didn't mean it was the truth. In a way, she was grateful to him, though that sounded ridiculous, but the man had truly made her grow up very fast, and she was a better mother for it.

Nick was hardly idealistic and didn't pretend to be.

Quite the opposite.

A hard realist with instincts that made a barracuda look cuddly, and a rock-hard approach to life that didn't give an inch of space if he didn't want to let it go.

She'd met men like him before—or had she? Of his ilk, maybe, but no one quite *like* him.

"My father liked you." She said the words to him, but looked straight out the windshield instead of *at* him.

"You sound surprised." Nick looked amused, expertly guiding the car into a different lane. "That's not exactly flattering."

"He doesn't like everyone," Reign informed him. "As a matter of fact, you should plaster a medal on your chest he even chose to talk to you."

"Any man courting another man's daughter has to face that firing squad."

She finally turned her head and considered him

from the passenger seat. "For someone who is living in this day and age, you choose some interesting language. Does anyone court anymore? I think we've done a bit beyond that."

She had a point, but Reign needed to understand he'd grown up with pretty old-fashioned beliefs. His mother would never be anything but pure Sicilian, and his father would skin him alive if he ever treated a woman with less than the utmost respect—God rest his soul.

An interesting standard, true, but a standard nonetheless.

Honor was always a non-negotiable facet to every personality. Nick thought it was probably as varied as the human species. He said, "We've slept together but that is entirely different from me courting you."

"Now we are really slipping back into the dark ages. You don't need to court me."

"Nice to know. You just fall into bed with every guy you meet? Because I bet most of them ask."

That ticked her off. "Of course I don't. Stop being an asshole."

"Ah, see, now we're on the same page." He didn't think that at all, but anger was better than her pensive expression when she'd left her father. He got it in spades, because to tell the truth, he'd rather have visited his father in prison than get the news he was dead, but he doubted it was easy.

She glared at him, and he had to admit that accusatory flare in her eyes was arousing.

Reign didn't do anything halfway. "*Is* that what you think?"

A dog ran across the road, and he swerved and wondered what the hell a dog was doing loose in this neighborhood. "Could we skip this argument?" he suggested. "I like you and I think you like me back. . . . We're all on the same page."

"Until you just suggested I was a slut."

"Lord, Reign, you know I did no such thing."

She was quiet for a few minutes, looking out over the sun setting across the Hudson River. Then she sighed. "You know the very worst part about sleeping with a guy?"

Nick had to choke down a laugh, but he was relieved her tone had calmed. "I can say with some authority that, no, I don't. Never slept with one. In case you haven't noticed, I like women."

She had the grace to grin. "Okay, maybe I phrased it wrong, but the trouble comes from the immediate sense of possession. Why is it not possible for a man to feel you are special and therefore different? I'd love to know what the fuck the problem is. You all do your best to get us into bed, and then you're outraged when we agree. Oh, you like it at the time, but once the blood returns to your brain, you start wondering if it wasn't such a big deal."

"Was it?"

The river was quiet except for a water authority boat cruising by and one lone tanker.

"Yes," she replied, staring out the window. "It

was a big deal, Nicky. But I'm going to tell you here and now, I don't deal well with issues of trust. Not on either side. I need to trust you, and you need to trust me, or it just doesn't work."

She looked . . . vulnerable. Very beautiful with her slender neck and remote profile and sleek dark hair, but also like someone he wanted to protect. It was taking him out of his comfort zone, and maybe he was not reacting in the right way, but surely he was allowed to have feelings as well.

It took him a minute but he admitted, "It was kind of a big deal for me too."

# SIXTEEN

She'd been right about the pasta.

As delicious as she remembered.

Driving back from dinner, he passed a taxi with easy expertise. Negotiating traffic in New York was definitely an acquired skill and took some fortitude.

"That was a nice dinner."

Reign agreed.

"I'm sorry we had the misunderstanding."

It was said in an emotionless tone, but she was starting to realize that Nick used that fairly ordinary tone often to disguise any semblance of deeper feeling, and maybe it was just as well. She was far too involved already with such an enigmatic man.

In her opinion, that he was approached to kill her and that was a catalyst to their relationship was not just a misunderstanding, but the conciliatory attempt was noted. She had the sense that he did not apologize easily.

To lighten the mood, she recounted her story of visiting the hospital. "At first, when the nurse told me his doctor was interested in Sal, I just thought it was kind of funny. Not because he isn't good-looking and smart, but because the nurse was having so much fun with it. Then I saw them together. . . . I think it is possible."

"Less competition for me."

"Hmm, he was never competition and don't flatter yourself either, because Sal and I split long before you—"

"We're being followed."

The terse interruption stopped her mid-sentence. "What?"

"Oh yeah." Nick switched lanes and glanced back in the rearview mirror. "Son of a bitch," he swore softly. "And he's good too. I can usually spot a tail pretty easily."

Reign had to admit her stomach tightened. "So what are you going to do?"

"If you weren't with me, I'd lead him somewhere isolated and if he had the guts to follow once he realized what I was doing, and I think this one might, we'd have ourselves a little conversation. But you *are* with me, so I think instead I am going to go visit a friend of mine."

"Who?"

"He might be able to help me out with this small problem, and luckily, he doesn't live too far away."

Obviously "who" was not going to be offered up and she didn't ask again. "All right. Can I do something?"

"Sit tight and hold on. I'd try and lose this guy, but you know, it would be much more satisfying to have him stick with me."

She put her hand on the side of the door as he whipped around a curve. "I'm just going to trust you."

Reign already had in many ways.

"Stay low, got it?"

"I'm not all that new to this game, Fattelli."

"A game like this?" The car accelerated and so did her pulse.

"Being followed? No, but don't sell me short. I meant I've tried to stay off the radar my entire life."

"Fuck." His gaze was fastened on the traffic but kept swiftly changing to the rearview mirror. "Sell you short? That I would never do. I'm going to press a number on my phone. Could you please tell the person who answers we are on our way? Just say my name."

She did it. The person who picked up was not full of surprise, and she hadn't heard an Irish accent that thick in quite some time. He asked one quick question once she identified herself as being with Nick Fattelli.

"Make and model of the car behind you?"

Nick said to her, "Black Buick and it's pretty new. Tell him we'll be at his place in ten minutes."

She did and signed off. Lights flashed by. "Who was that?"

"Pat."

"Pat who?"

"We aren't going to go into details." Nick didn't

precisely run a light but he first slowed and then sped through it as if at the last minute he decided he had time, and murmured, "If they find us at his place, we are going to know a few things."

Patrick Stevens was not Italian, but hey, no one was perfect. He was a thickset older man that might remind a person of someone who could dig ditches or toss trash into a truck, but he was the single quickest mind when it came to surveillance that Nick had ever met, and absolutely ruthless. He answered the door to his brownstone wearing jeans so faded they were almost white and a Jets jersey.

"What do we have?"

"Not quite sure. Catch the tail as it swings by?"

"Done." Pat stared at Reign as Nick practically dragged her inside. Well, she was worth staring at, especially in a little red number that resembled a cocktail dress but was a bit skimpy on the skirt length. His friend said, "I think I can guess why. I'd follow her too."

"Someone has tried to kill her twice."

"Now that would be a damn shame. I am usually partial to blondes but a little variety never hurt anyone."

Nick said smoothly, "I couldn't agree more. Run the plate when the car comes by, okay? He was behind us, but he'll circle back around the block, I promise you."

"You're the expert on that. Sure. But we should hurry."

Reign, Nick had to admit, looked a little flabbergasted by the interior of Pat's house. It really consisted of walls of televisions and monitors and audio equipment. If she had a clue as to the arsenal in the basement, even coming from her background, she might faint.

Well, no, maybe not. Reign would never faint. She didn't even comment on the mess in the living room, which consisted of dirty plates, empty beer cans, and stacks of DVDs. Pat had some reclusive habits.

"Not a lot of Bentleys in this neighborhood, so he'll spot yours. . . ." Pat studied a wall of screens and pointed. "Okay, this your guy? He's driving a little slow past your vehicle now."

*Sure enough, that same black car. . . .*

"Fuck yes, that's him."

"I'll photograph the plate." Pat pushed a button. "Done. If someone far . . . I mean, sneezes on this street, I know about it."

"How fast can you run it?"

"About a minute. I'm linked into the state database."

"Do they know that?"

"You know better than to ask questions like that, Fattelli." The screen flashed. "Here's the registration. Rental. Must be pros. How good were they?"

"I noticed them." Nick didn't like it. At all.

"Yeah, but you're good too, Fattelli. Give me a scale so I can place them." Pat swiveled his chair and picked up a glass of iced tea. "Like how soon would the average person have noticed?"

"Maybe never," he admitted, a little cold inside. Reign stood next to him and he slipped an arm around her waist. "That good. What the hell is up?"

"I'm going to guess from the make of the car and the skill of the driver, there's some money behind it." Pat hit a few more keys. "I might be able to get the names but I doubt they are real enough to mean anything."

It wasn't like anything Nick hadn't already guessed. So his beautiful evening had just turned to shit. . . .

"Can you check my car?"

"For a signal? Sure."

Reign leaned her head on Nick's shoulder. It was hardly a characteristic gesture, and he tightened his hold protectively.

"Okay," Pat said in triumph, grinning. "We do have a passenger. Your fancy British import has a device attached somewhere. I don't touch foreign cars so you'll have to find it yourself."

And he'd thought it was Reign's phone. Nick did a regroup. That was a serious mistake on his part.

"They tagged my car with a GPS? By the way, I'm not sure the Brits pass as imports."

Pat looked pained. "Looks like it's about the GPS, and we went our separate ways a couple of centuries ago. Can you ever remember I'm Irish? My mother was an O'Brien from Northern Ireland. It's Saturday-night entertainment to us to blow up highbrow Brit cars like yours."

Following Pat's train of thought wasn't particularly simple. Nick said, "Fine, I won't make you touch a British car if you hold a grudge."

"Oh yeah, a Sicilian wouldn't know about that. Have you ever heard of a vendetta? I kind of think you people invented that."

"Heard of it once or twice, now that you mention it. Thanks, by the way."

"Rear bumper would be my guess, or the inside of one of the tire wells. If you'd like to just leave the lady here, I'll take care of her—"

"Helpful. And no, she stays with me. I don't want to lose her to all that Irish charm."

"There is a true danger there." Pat grinned and took Reign's hand, kissed it, and said in an exaggerated brogue, "It's been a pleasure, lassie."

"Nice to meet you, Pat."

"Watch it." Nick turned in the doorway. "I'm going to toss it when I find it, so they might come looking for us here."

Pat shrugged. "Biggest mistake they ever made if that is how it goes."

Once they were back outside, Nick slipped out a small flashlight he always carried from his pocket and opened the passenger door for Reign. "Get in while I try to solve our little problem."

He found it fairly easily on the left-hand tire well, the tiny light making it not that difficult if a person was at all suspicious, and God knew he was suspicious as hell now. He slid into the driver's seat and took great pleasure in tossing the device out the window when they pulled away.

"Hopefully it will get stuck in the tire of a police cruiser and lead them to the nearest precinct." Nick was still wary, driving slowly, since it was getting late and it was a quiet neighborhood. He didn't think they'd risk anything where there could be witnesses. It was hard to tell, but if they were waiting to make a move, hopefully they'd think they were still inside the house, relying on the tracking device.

Once they turned randomly onto a different street, he breathed a little easier. "You know, before this little incident, I was kind of thinking this might be Ariano's problem instead of yours."

Reign turned to stare at him. "Sal? Why?"

He shrugged. "Think about it. You were involved with him before me. It makes sense that if a man was in your bedroom, Ariano would be the one there. Let's also keep in mind that he was the one shot twice on his parents' yacht."

Nick took three more turns in rapid succession and then turned on his own GPS to get them back to the street they needed.

No comment on that theory. At least not at first. Finally, as they pulled out into traffic she said, "I suppose it is possible. His father has enemies, but I think everyone I know does anyway. I can't think why anyone else would want to hurt someone like Sal."

"He's going to be a lawyer, for Christ's sake, Reign. If someone is responsible for putting me away, I am going to hate his guts."

"He isn't a lawyer quite yet though, and it isn't like he's going to be a prosecutor or anything. That would be ironic, wouldn't it, if he chose that path, but he won't." Her tone was dry. "But my point is, I don't see it as a viable theory. Sal is at school every day with a predictable schedule. Look at your friend Pat. He could find out when Sal's classes were, and where, with no trouble. Two seconds max."

"I'm not sure I would classify Pat as a friend. Let's leave it as interesting and useful acquaintance, can we?"

But maybe she was right. He consciously loosened his jaw.

He just didn't want the target to be *her*. These people, whoever they were, seemed to be trying fairly hard to pull this off.

Over his dead body.

Reign reached over and lightly touched his knee and echoed that thought. "I'm just wondering, could it be *you* they are after?"

# SEVENTEEN

T he hotel was downtown in the middle of a chic neighborhood, the towering structure studded with lights, and the doorman was probably dressed more impeccably than most of the guests as he came to open the car door for Reign. "Checking in?"

She stepped out, assaulted by the city, a mixture of exhaust and the noise of the traffic, and of course, the almost overwhelming array of fashionable buildings.

The hotel in particular was an icon in the history of New York, and even America in general.

Nick nodded and discreetly handed him a bill. "If you'll take care of the car please. No porter necessary. We have no luggage."

"No problem, sir." The man looked absolutely bland and accepted the keys to the Bentley.

As Nick took Reign's arm, she murmured, "Uhm,

that whole no-luggage thing is kind of a problem." Then she added, "Nice choice. I've never stayed here. Have you?"

He escorted her into the brilliantly lit lobby without answering the question. It was the epitome of understated good taste, with scattered seating areas and plants with glossy perfect leaves. The paintings on the walls and the sculptures were undoubtedly museum quality.

If money had a smell, this was the scent in the air.

"If you're worried about what you'll wear to bed, the answer is nothing, so it all seems good to me on the luggage issue." Nick glanced around and then urged her toward the very discreet desk to check in.

"Very funny."

"Oh, I'm dead serious about that. But I need some time to think in a place where I'm not worried we'll be found."

"I get that. But I at least need a toothbrush."

"I'm pretty sure you can get anything you want here just by asking."

"What if they can trace your credit card?" Reign looked outwardly composed but he could tell she was at least a bit shaken.

He said ironically, "You think I don't have that covered?"

"Oh."

Pat wasn't the only one interested in how she looked in her red dress, he noticed as he gave the front desk his information—not any of it attached to the name Fattelli. Luckily, they were able to get a suite on a high floor, and while the evening hadn't exactly worked out as he'd thought it would, the ending would hopefully be just as enjoyable as the beginning had been.

He'd very much liked sitting across from Reign at the table at the restaurant, watching the light play off the planes of her face, shadowing her eyes, but it seemed like each time they went anywhere disaster lurked, and now she'd brought up a pretty valid point.

On the whole, he probably had more enemies than she did.

Blaming it on her famous family name didn't work either.

He was starting to think she could be right. Maybe he was the target.

It might make sense. He was the first one shot at in her bedroom. At the time, he'd thought maybe it was because taking the male out of the equation first was advisable, but now he wondered. He'd also been standing next to her before Ariano took his place, and from the water, the visibility might have been a little dicey. Maybe they had thought the tall man with her was him.

Tonight, it was definitely *his* car that was tagged, which was why they were at a hotel instead of his apartment.

It was entirely possible that he'd been sucked in because someone wanted him there. The whole offer to kill Reign might have been just to position him into place so he could be removed from the picture.

He was starting to think it was the way the game was slated to be played, but he had not been given the opportunity to suit up.

They took the elevator to the eleventh floor and the hallway was quiet and cool. He took the key card, swiped the door, and let Reign inside. "Let me order up some champagne and a couple of glasses."

"Mind telling me what we're celebrating?" She turned around and put her hands on her hips.

There was no doubt she looked gorgeous when irritated.

"Not being shot at *again*?" he suggested. "I somehow think that might have been on our agenda this evening."

She had the most beautiful mouth. He was fascinated, even though he should probably have been a lot more worried about the men who were out there wondering how they'd lost his car—hopefully.

"Could they have been FBI agents?" she asked.

"I haven't done anything illegal lately." He moved toward the table and the phone. "You?"

"Oh, seriously?"

"Is that a yes or a no?"

"That is an 'I am going to kick your ass if we ever have to have this conversation again.' Yes, I've committed a crime recently. I really should never have designed that dress with fringe on the hem, but I did it anyway. That's a crime. Call me impulsive. Fashion citation, right there. Fringe, right? Who am I? Pocahontas? Otherwise, no. Under the definition of the laws of the state of New York, nothing illegal.

Well, I parked in a loading zone for about six minutes the other day. Sue me."

"You are pretty hot when you are mad."

"I was under the impression I was hot all the time."

The way her tone had altered spelled a better ending for his up-and-down evening. He punched in the numbers on the phone and asked for a very— *very*—expensive bottle of champagne, charged it to the room, and then hung up and took off his coat. "When room service knocks, let me answer the door. One never knows."

"I've heard that before." Reign dropped into a chair. "You know, I sometimes wonder how I signed on for this rollercoaster ride."

"You and me both." He discarded his tie in a careless toss. "But, truth be told, I think I might find being a minister boring. Not that they aren't good people. I'm just saying."

"That would be the church of what?" For the first time since he'd found the GPS, she finally laughed.

"I have to admit I am unsure of the denomination myself."

"Yes, well, that might be a church that all those who seek redemption might want to avoid." Her voice altered. "What do we do now?"

"We drink champagne and make love. Then fall deeply asleep."

"My son—"

"Reign, I think we've both figured out this isn't

about that sort of thing. They either want you, or maybe you're not it and they want me. I'm very aware of Vince, but you've called and warned him, not to mention passing on the message through your father. There isn't one part of me that does not think the minute we walked out of that prison, your father wasn't pulling strings."

"Tell me about yours."

Why had he been afraid all along they would have to have this conversation?

"Italian men talk about their mothers. We leave our fathers out of it. Don't you know anything?" He moved and checked the window. The street looked clear.

"So he's dead. I wondered."

"Look—" He started to tell her that perhaps they should just change the subject, but her gaze was sympathetic and he wanted her and . . . oh hell, this was apparently really complicated.

Nick took in a deep breath. "I saw you with your father today and it brought back a few memories. I loved mine, he was killed when I was nineteen, and I don't want to talk about it. My brother is a priest and even he and I don't discuss it, so don't be insulted."

She glanced around the expensive hotel room and her voice was even. "I'm not. You and I are getting to know each other. I thought I had something special with my ex-husband, but the truth wasn't really all that important to him. Prove to me you value it."

It was either the worst—or the best—time for someone to knock on the door.

Nick deftly uncorked the champagne himself after tipping and graciously dismissing the young man who had brought the room-service cart. Reign watched him do it, the fluid motion effortless, and he poured her a glass first—he had good manners, that was undisputed—and handed it over.

*Here I am,* she thought as she took the glass, *playing with fire again.* No one knew where she was. Oh sure, if she disappeared, Nick would come under scrutiny, but then again, he'd registered them under an assumed name.

But he'd saved her ass more than once as far as she could tell, and he was . . . exciting.

Dangerous.

"Shall we toast?"

He looked at her and picked up his glass. The tiny bubbles frothed the surface of the liquid inside it. "To?"

"Making love and drinking champagne."

"Not a bad choice. Take off your clothes first."

She had to admit that was a unique approach. "Excuse me?"

"I want to sit here and drink champagne with you naked." Before she could speak he lifted a hand in a placating gesture. "Just a request. If you don't want to, don't. I know enough about you that it has registered you don't like orders."

"I hate them actually." She toed off a shoe.

"Uhm." He watched it hit the floor, his untouched drink in his hand. "That's a nice start. Mind if I sit and enjoy the show?"

"I think you've got a voyeurism thing going, Fattelli." She leaned over—gave him a really nice view of her breasts—and slipped off the other shoe.

"I like looking at you, what can I say?"

"You like my tits." She sat up and swung back her dark hair.

"Don't forget that world-class ass." He lounged lower in his chair.

"Even Pat could have come up with a more charming comment than that one."

He grinned, and it was, she had to admit, pretty effective. Boyish, yet also somehow entirely grownup, hungry male. "Hey, it was a compliment, and don't try and make me jealous."

"Would you be?" She was just curious.

"Hell yes, but I'm assuming Pat is not really a threat."

She surveyed his athletic build and handsome face and had to admit, Pat hardly measured up, but she informed him, "On a superficial level, no."

He set the bottle back in the ice bucket. "Are you telling me it is the intellect that matters?"

"The whole package."

"Okay. How am I doing so far?"

Interesting question. There was no doubt he was capable, courteous, good-looking, all balanced with enough intrigue that appealed to her adventurous side. . . .

Instead of answering directly, she shot back, "I'm thirsty, so I'll indulge your little fantasy. Unzip me?" she stood and turned her back.

"Those words, when they come from you, are music to my ears. My pleasure." He came over and obliged.

The pleasure was all hers as his mouth pressed the nape of her neck, and he lowered the zipper on her dress with excruciating care, taking his time, then pushing the garment finally off her shoulders. Reign leaned back against him, feeling the strength and heat of his body, as his hands came around, first to unfasten her bra, sliding it off her arms, then to cup her breasts.

"I do love these. I suppose I'm guilty as charged there." His breath was warm against her neck and his fingers did some very nice things. "I've never been able to decide if I am a breast man or a leg man."

"I thought we were going to toast?"

"We are. Lose the thong, sweetheart." His hands slid to her hips. "I'll be happy to help."

Even as she shimmied out of it, she said, "Now see, that sounded like an order."

He let go and backed away. "It wasn't meant to be. When it comes to you, I sometimes lose track of my train of thought."

She had to confess the same problem, even if she didn't do it out loud. She settled back on the chair totally nude now, the tautness of her nipples no doubt revealing her own arousal. She picked up her glass in a languid movement. "Here's to fine champagne and making love. Did I get that right?"

"Almost. Don't cross your legs."

He was enormously aroused. She could see the bulge in those finely tailored trousers, and her body responded traitorously, the heat between her legs building. Deliberately, she did as he requested, opening her legs a little so he could see her sex and notice, no doubt, that she was already wet.

Nick said, "Here's to drinking champagne and having wild sex with the most intriguing woman I have ever met."

The word "love" made her uncomfortable also, so she leaned forward and touched her glass to his in a light, delicate clink.

The champagne was perfect, light and crisp, and she had no doubt he'd paid quite a lot for it. They both drank, and then she eyed him over the rim of her glass. "What are you going to do about the current problem that we aren't sure is mine or yours?"

"Not worry about it tonight." His blue eyes were intently focused on her nude body. "Tomorrow is, after all, another day. I'll make some calls, sniff around, and see if I have a problem I'm not aware of, but for now my attention is focused elsewhere."

"I think I can guess where."

His response held a hint of moody resentment. "You know, I find you too distracting."

A very telling statement. Outside, the skyline was like a canopy of jeweled light, and there was the slight hint of traffic moving below, but it was all background. Reign waited a moment. "How much is too much?"

"Let's say if the door was being battered down I still might fuck you before I assessed the problem. That qualifies as too distracted."

She drained her glass. "I don't know that I ever agreed you could fuck me."

"Sweetheart, you are naked and drinking champagne in our hotel room. We both know I'm going to fuck you, and I am happy to say from gratifying previous experience, you are going to fuck me right back."

With a provocative lift of her brows, she shot back, "Maybe. I'm kind of getting tired of waiting if you want the truth."

"Jesus, I'm not fifteen." Nick stood and started to undress. A shoe hit the wall as he tossed it carelessly. "But you do drive me a little crazy."

He was beautiful in his own right, she thought as he stripped, his torso gleaming in the reflected light, all defined muscle and sinew, his profile clean and masculine.

Not to mention the size of his swollen cock when he discarded his pants. He stalked over to where she sat—there was no other way to describe it—and said, "You can walk to the bed or I can pick you up and take you there, but either way, this is the equation: my cock and your tight pussy. Got it?"

"Bossy," she murmured as she rose in a smooth movement.

"Tease," he said in response and physically picked her up. "Carrying it is."

"I would have walked."

"I'm not in the mood for a long wait."

"I wouldn't—"

He kissed her, effectively ending the conversation.

# EIGHTEEN

Even in the grip of what was a feverish sexual need that startled him with its intensity, Nick instinctively made sure he chose the side of the bed where he'd set his Glock on the nightstand so it was within reach.

Apparently even the hard-on of the century couldn't deflect that habit.

"Let's do this a little differently." Reign's voice had taken on a just-slightly-lower tone he had discovered he liked to hear. A lot.

"You enjoy playing with my body, let me play with yours." She got to her knees next to him on the bed, her long hair a contrast to her smooth skin.

He settled on his back. "There's an offer I can't refuse."

A slow smile curved her mouth. "Just don't forget me."

"I can't seem to," he responded more softly than

he intended, looking into her eyes. "And just so we're clear, that is very, very unusual."

"I'm not looking for a commitment." Her hand drifted down his chest and her lashes lowered.

"I'm not offering one." He sucked in a breath as she ran a finger down the length of his cock.

In the back of his mind the word "yet" lingered, but luckily what she was doing at the moment distracted him from wondering if he'd lost his mind.

"So smooth and hot." Reign began to give him a hand job, slow and with just enough pressure it threatened his control but didn't quite send him over the edge. Perfect. The sensation was so pleasurable he wasn't interested in having it over anytime soon. His left hand was fisted in the bedspread and he had to consciously relax.

Nick closed his eyes. "Sweet Jesus, you do that nearly as well as I do."

She gently squeezed the tip of his cock. "Is that a compliment?"

"It is. Lord, if you keep doing that, this will be over pretty soon."

She laughed, low and throaty, and leaned over to kiss him. Against his lips she murmured, "I was kind of hoping for a long night."

"I'm pretty sure you could ask me for anything right now. Besides, did you see how many condoms I tossed on the bed?"

"Yeah, that was pretty promising."

Nick opened his eyes and brushed back her hair behind her ear in an intimate gesture. He loved the way her hair smelled, like lilacs in the spring, clean and fresh, and the sensation of it brushing his chest was beyond erotic. "Care to put one on me so we can continue this with a little more fun for you?"

She did as he asked, kneeling there like a lush goddess, and the moment he was covered, he rolled her to her back, moving on top of her. "My turn?" he asked. "I'm feeling a little selfish so far."

"Help yourself."

It was no secret he was a fan of her breasts and he started there, nibbling and sucking and holding the pliant flesh in his hands, trying to at least show some measure of patience.

Lucky for him, Reign was not long on patience, especially in bed. "If you wouldn't mind fucking me, sometime in the next decade would be good. Men always think foreplay is essential to women, but it can be overrated. Put that"—she stroked his rigid cock and pointed at her pussy—"here."

The graphic suggestion as she opened her legs and pointed made him catch her hands and pull them over her head. Nick asked roughly, "Like this?"

Immediately he was worried he'd been too rough when she gave a small cry after he entered her with a slick, hard thrust.

He stilled, suddenly aware with an acute sense of how much smaller she was than him despite those voluptuous curves. "Good?"

"Are you kidding me? Yes. If you stop, I'll kill you." She stared up at him fiercely and wrapped her legs around his waist.

"You do realize *you* are the bossy one." With exquisite sensation bombarding him, it was a little hard to get the words out.

Her nails bit into his shoulders.

He decided if the lady was that impatient . . .

She was, he found out, moving with him in a fluent rhythm they'd seemed to have in common from that very first encounter, as if while they might be getting to know each other intellectually on a cautious basis, their bodies had thrown that caution to the four winds and recognized the attraction.

The damn woman was like a drug, and he was addicted.

He couldn't say who came first. All he knew was that in the aftermath they lay in each other's arms, and he could literally feel the pounding of her heart against his chest. Or was it his?

Both maybe. He struggled to take a breath and thankfully succeeded.

Though if he were to die, this was how he'd want to go.

Reign smoothed his hair back, her body soft and pliant beneath him. "Okay, all is well with the world." She added, "At least at this moment."

"I agree."

But they still needed to consider their next move, and he was always proactive, always thinking and moving forward. He'd stayed alive because of his ability to do so, and things seemed to be heating up.

"Tomorrow morning I'll order room service and over breakfast, maybe we can sort this out, one-on-one."

"Try to decide if it is you or me, right?"

Nick stroked her cheek, letting his fingers feather down her throat. "I'm not going to let anyone near you."

"I hate to inform you of this, but I might be the one to not let anyone hurt *you*."

Fierce was entirely appropriate.

"Do you ever give an inch?" He had to laugh.

"Not very often, though I like when you do. . . . And when you give, it is definitely more than an inch." She lifted her hips.

"Reign, I'm being serious."

"Me too."

"Tomorrow morning. It's a date."

"And what would you call this?" She stirred in his arms.

"An even better kind of date."

"I need this to be resolved because of Vince."

"I've always wanted to be a father."

The words just escaped—he was older than she was, and he did to a certain extent envy that she had a son. He'd waited and she hadn't. She must have been a very beautiful young mother.

Way too honest. Even he wasn't sure where that came from. He wasn't sure how to fix it either, but Reign must have took pity on him, because she just said evenly after reading his expression, "It isn't the world's easiest job, so not for the faint of heart."

"I'm sure not." Dissembling seemed the best course, especially since he'd never planned to be so open in the first place. "But for the sake of argument, do I seem faint of heart?"

Reign had always wanted for Vince to understand that life consisted of a variety of choices, but she wasn't sure she'd always made the right ones—well, it was obvious she hadn't since she was now divorced—and so preaching at her son had never been an option. She was very happy he'd been admitted into a good university and hoped he'd make a go of it, and she was willing to work her ass off to make sure he had the chance.

This affair had come at the worst time possible, especially if Nick Fattelli was dragging along some baggage in the form of someone who wanted him dead. Or maybe she was the intended victim. . . . Or was it Sal? She had no idea.

With Nicky's rangy body pinning hers to the bed, she could hardly start a good argument, and she didn't even want one. Reign placed her palm on his bare chest. "No, your heart seems to be functioning just fine."

"Your son is grown and I'm not asking you to have my baby." Nick's smile could lure a stone angel off an ancient Roman church. "I was just saying, we are getting to know each other and I thought I'd share. I always wanted to be a father."

"Where the hell were you when I was a teenaged girl wondering about sex?"

"Learning about sex from women a little bit older than me."

He stood and went into the bathroom, and she

heard the toilet flush as he got rid of the condom. He came out nude and looking fairly relaxed for a man who'd been followed through a good portion of the city earlier by unknown people who might just want to kill him.

As a bonus, he brought the only half-empty bottle of champagne and refilled their glasses.

Nick slid into the bed and said calmly as he handed her the flute, "I was fifteen my first time and she was quite a bit older. I'm not going to say how much older or who she was, but wow. She was not a pedophile, for the record. I told her I was nineteen and I looked it. She had no idea it was my first time but I think she got the drift once we got into bed and it was over pretty fast. It was a one-performance deal." He glanced over in amusement. "I've never told anyone else this story, by the way, since it is kind of humiliating. Now you go."

Humiliating that he'd caught the eye of an attractive older woman? Reign could easily see how it would happen. He was noticeable. No doubt about it.

She drew the sheet up around her. "What is this? Like war stories or something?"

"Pillow talk. Just tell me."

Oh, what the hell. It was hardly a deep dark secret. "I met Vince's dad very young. Grade school. It was a sweet romance that graduated to something more, and eventually we were teenagers groping in the backseat. We got married so young—my parents had to sign a paper to allow it, and we had

Vince within the first year. I was, to say the least . . . idealistic. My father was not at all happy about Ray, but I can be determined if I want something."

"I've noticed the independent streak. What happened next?"

"He was irresponsible and a liar." That was more than kind. Her ex-husband was out of her life.

"Not a good combination." Nick lifted his glass to his mouth in a natural masculine movement, broad shoulders relaxed against the pillows.

He was right. She agreed, "Not for our marriage and not for our child."

"But Vince sounds great."

"He's pretty centered. Most of the time." Reign had to take in a breath. The fine sheets were heavy against the sensitive tips of her breasts. "I don't even know why I'm talking about it. Why do I feel so comfortable with you?"

It was a true question, even if the setting was a very posh—but by definition generic—hotel room in Manhattan somewhere. Soft sheets, soft lighting, a view of the city . . . all of that did not matter to her, and the man had openly admitted he was asked to kill her.

This was the strangest romance known to mankind—but it was still a romance.

He sent her a look out of those vivid blue eyes. "How am I supposed to answer that question?"

"Your thoughts might be nice. Try."

"Try? I'm not impartial. Drink some champagne and let me think about it."

Part of it was, she knew, this easy sense of companionship, as if they were two people who understood each other more than anyone understood either of them. Who he was didn't really bother her any longer. At first, yes, but she was getting over it.

How she felt about him did bother her, though.

It scared her more than a little.

He tentatively began: "I think we're great in bed together."

"I'm tossing that guy answer right out."

"Reign, I'm a *guy*. Ask me a question and you are likely to get a guy answer." There was open exasperation in his voice.

Fine, he had a point.

She took in a deep, deep breath. "I'm trying to make sense of getting involved with someone who I know is bad for me. Been there, done that. I'm smarter now than that girl who made that mistake."

"Bad in what way? Am I really a mistake? Tell me how."

Good question. But not one she was really ready to answer. Her voice broke. "I don't know, Nicky. I want my son safe. I want my career, and I'd also like to stay alive to make both of those things happen."

To her surprise he put his glass aside and put his arms around her. "Let me take care of it, and before you argue, we can talk about this over our breakfast date tomorrow morning, remember?"

"All we ever seem to do is eat together and make . . . and have sex."

His mouth brushed her temple. "What the hell do most people do? Long walks on the beach? Watch the sunset at Key West? Ride a Ferris wheel holding hands? All that sometimes happens, but the truth is, not every damn day. This evening we took a lovely drive through the city, doesn't that count?"

She pushed at his chest, laughing. "Uhm, I believe we were eluding a car containing someone following us—I doubt because he wanted to sell us a magazine subscription."

"At least I made you laugh." He picked up his glass again and lounged back against the pillows.

Maybe that was it. He did make her laugh. And smile. And at the right times moan, because however it started, he was right, he was very good in bed. But it wasn't enough. There was more depth to this man, but he wasn't interested in letting it show. Reign asked as offhandedly as possible, "So tell me about your brother, the priest."

"He's a priest, Reign. I don't know what specifically you are asking. Obviously unmarried, no kids, devotes his life to the church. John seems happy enough with it, but it certainly wouldn't be for me."

What an understatement that was. A hit man with a brother who is a priest? At least now she knew his brother's name.

She took a sip. "Hmm. You two get along?"

Nick seemed to consider his answer. "We're obviously not very much alike, but he's family. We get along. We have an understanding. I don't confess my sins and he doesn't ask about them either. Seems to work for us. Where's the remote?"

"My sister is my best friend. We'd walk through fire for each other and she adores Vince."

"Another interesting Reign Grazi fact I'll place in the file. Want to watch late-night television?"

"Any sisters?"

"Can we stop this probing into my life? It isn't all that interesting."

Okay, she'd struck a nerve. It wasn't intentional, but he asked about *her* life frequently enough.

She took in his slightly moody expression with a woman's intuition. "This from a man who doesn't like pate? Who doesn't like pate?"

"Me." He eyed the glass in her hand. "Now finish your drink like a good girl and I'll reward you."

"With?"

He took the glass away before she finished the last sip and rolled on top of her, his erection pressing her thigh, murmuring, "Something I have come to the conclusion you like very much."

"Oh, what's that?"

"Fucking."

She theatrically lowered her lashes. "If you continue to be so romantic, I could hardly refuse you."

At that moment he hesitated, and that really was not like him. "What if I was more romantic?"

The intense look in his eyes threw her off balance. "I think you're confusing romance with physical attraction."

"I thought that was what you might say."

"And I think *you're* changing the subject by deflecting me with sexual advances, Mr. Fattelli."

"Is it working?" He nibbled on her earlobe, which seemed to be a skill he'd mastered quite well at some point in his life.

She was both a little annoyed over the secrecy but also interested. He got an erection faster than any man she'd ever had an intimate relationship with in her life. That same virility was no doubt part of why he could take charge of a situation so swiftly. "Seems to be. Roll over."

"If you insist." He complied with a lazy smile and athletic male grace. "I like it with the lady on top, no doubt about it."

"I'm a woman, and in bed no lady, as I'm sure you've noticed." She slipped out of bed and went to pick up his silk tie from where it was draped over the side of a chair. "This is just a little variation on the theme. Lift your arms."

He also lifted his brows, but obligingly put his hands above his head. Of course when she straddled him and began to loop the material around his wrists, he rose up enough to lick the underside of her breast in a wicked sweep of his tongue. "Tying me to the bed? I'm intrigued, but I thought you liked how I use my hands."

"Oh, I do." The elegant headboard was a bit of a challenge but she managed to thread the ends of the tie through the intricate metalwork and secure the ends. Reign had no illusions that if he wanted to free himself, he probably could, but this was more about sensual trust than anything.

Apparently emotional trust was a ways off, but in this medium they communicated very well.

His eyes gleamed with arousal and that was hardly the only evidence. His cock was hard against the flat plane of his belly and when Reign leaned down to lightly run her tongue along the tip, his body visibly jerked.

"Jesus." He said it through clenched teeth when she merely sat back on his thighs and smiled. "If you tied me up to just torture me—"

Reign leaned over. "You know me better than that. I just need a condom. Do you mind if I do the honors?"

"I don't think there's a lot of choice on my end. I'm tied up, remember."

"Your end is nice, but I like your front best." She peeled off the wrapper and rolled it slowly down his erection, taking her time about it.

"Ms. Reign, you have quite the sense of humor. Bring that pussy here since I can't come to it." His skin had a sheen of sweat that betrayed he wasn't as self-possessed as he seemed.

Fine with her. She loved it when he lost it, because when a person checked on the definition of badass, she was fairly sure Nick Fattelli's name was on that list.

So she deliberately drove him crazy.

First lowering herself onto his cock until he had fully sheathed it and then moving up so he slid almost free and kissing him like an inexperienced girl, no tongue, just a press of her lips, her palms braced on his chest.

"That feels good," she said with feigned shyness.

Then she did it again.

"I'm only going to let you get away with this for so long," he said thickly. "Just giving you a word of warning."

She sank back down, and it wasn't that desire was like fire licking through her veins, but he was usually so in control it was an intriguing change of pace. "All bets off?"

"All of them."

She moved then, faster and harder, the up and down motions as she rode him rapidly and it was gratifying when he came first, his orgasm spiraling into hers as he powerfully lifted his hips time and again.

His hands, she discovered, were untied already and smoothed down her bare back as she lay on his chest. He said, "Reign, you do know you make me crazy, right?"

# NINETEEN

He'd been awake since five but finally fallen back asleep after brushing his teeth, which wasn't so easy one-handed, since his shoulder was still pretty painful. Sal contemplated making some coffee but opted for a pain pill instead, then lay in bed sweating until he finally drifted off.

That party was over when he woke up.

He rolled over and groaned.

It was very much better to be in his bed than in the hospital, but it was hardly perfect.

First of all, sitting up was a real problem. He didn't have a nurse to come at the press of a button either, and he'd ignored the instructions to have someone come stay with him.

Reign would have been his first choice anyway, and she was probably with Fattelli. *Just as well,* he thought as he rolled out of bed in just his boxers. He could maybe defend another human being from a weak kitten. Some inconsiderate person seemed to be hammering on his door. If Reign was in danger and this person wanted in, he'd not be of much help since a single shove could send him to the floor.

When he jerked the door open, it wasn't an assassin on the other side. It was Dr. Altea, dressed for work in the usual pale blue scrubs but carrying a basket of some kind. Her hair was loose and soft around her oval face, and her topaz eyes were inquiring. "Welcome or not? I brought breakfast. Looks like I just got you out of bed. It's after nine. I thought I was safe."

The sun was brightly shining, illuminating the vines growing on the stucco walls of the private entrance to his condo. The air smelled like summer also, warm and fragrant.

He glanced down. "Oh hell, I'm in my underwear. Sorry, I'm a little groggy."

"I hate to mention this, but it's nothing I haven't seen before, so we're all good, but only if you want me here." She had a nice laugh, light and musical.

Why not? He'd sent a brief text to tell his parents he'd been released the night before, and he had mentioned he was tired. He loved his mother but wasn't in the mood to have her hovering over him. But *this* arrival was most welcome, if a little unexpected.

"Come on in." He stepped back. "Excuse me for a minute and I'll at least go put on pants."

"If it makes you more comfortable, but don't bother on my account." She walked in carrying a cardboard tray with two cups of what smelled like amazing coffee.

"I realize you've seen all my important parts in their dubious glory," he said dryly, "but I—"

She interrupted, slightly raising her brows. "And I was impressed."

It took him a moment to figure out how to respond to that flirtatious comment. Eventually, he found his voice. "Flattery will get you everywhere, Dr. Altea, but I guess I'm more old-fashioned than I thought, not wanting to have a cup of coffee with a lady in my Skivvies. Though don't count on a shirt. I still can't lift my arm very far. Luckily, I don't feel like going anywhere anyway, so I guess I'll just wander around here half-dressed until things get better."

"They will. I'll take a look and change the bandages before I leave."

"I'm a big boy, I follow the instructions. Besides, I didn't think doctors made house calls anymore."

"Neither did I. Wow, this is a nice place. Kitchen?"

It *was* nice. It belonged to someone his father knew who didn't ever use it, because he spent a lot of time down in Miami, and Sal rented it for a song on a caretaker kind of basis. It had tall windows letting in lots of light, leather furniture that had probably cost a small fortune, polished bamboo floors, a built-in bar, and Oriental rugs in bright colors. Sal suspected the paintings on the walls together were worth more than most people's houses. He'd never used the dining room that seated twelve. "Thanks. To your left. I'll be right back."

He went into his bedroom and fished out an old pair of worn sweatpants, decided they were good enough, and managed to get them on with minimal twinges.

When he walked into the kitchen, he saw Jennifer Altea had found the toaster and was putting in a bagel. There were small containers of cream cheese and butter on the counter, as well as what looked like a very nice bowl of fruit salad and a small jug of orange juice.

He liked how she moved. Graceful but efficient. As his doctor, he'd appreciated her brisk, no-nonsense honesty when she was treating him, but there was also a woman in there, and at the moment, he appreciated that even more. He leaned against the granite counter. "Can I help?"

She glanced over her shoulder. "Plates and silverware?"

"Oh, good idea." He had to grin as he moved to open the cupboard above the six-burner stove he rarely used. "I eat pizza with my hands in front of the television pretty often. Student thing."

"I'd yell at you about that, but I was guilty of it too. Doctors preach good nutrition, but we are pretty bad about it, always cutting corners due to time. Living in New York helps, since we have a lot of take-out choices, but I shudder when I think of the sodium content in most foods. To control that, you just have to cook for yourself. I hope you like green chile."

"Spicy is fine with me."

"These are green-chile bagels. I discovered them when I did a rotation at a hospital in Albuquerque,

New Mexico. I've never found them anywhere else, but there's a shop downtown here that offers them. So good." She hovered over the toaster. "Like heaven."

They *smelled* good, he had to admit. For dinner the night before he'd eaten a can of soup, which Reign had found in the pantry and heated up for him, but he'd barely been able to finish that, so anything geared toward finer cuisine would have been lost on him anyway. Sal also retrieved placemats from the drawer, and at least he was capable of setting the antique table by the big window with an impressive view, even if he did it one-handed.

It occurred to him that he didn't spend nearly enough time enjoying the wonderful space, but then again, time was a commodity he didn't have a lot of anyway.

He had to admit the bagels were fantastic. "All right, I'm a fan," he said after the first two butter-drenched bites. "Like seriously."

"I know." She ate with equal relish and he had to wonder, considering she was pretty slender, how often she took the time to sit down for a meal, just like him. The unusual color of her eyes intrigued him as she regarded him across the table. "For whatever reason, I just thought you'd be someone who would appreciate them."

"Mental connection?"

She took a bite and chewed and swallowed before she answered. "Maybe. I'm thinking it might be more a physical attraction right now."

Sal choked on his sip of coffee. When he recovered, he said, "I can roll with that, but are you always so blunt?"

"I'd ask how you could afford a place like this, but I'm afraid to hear the answer. Your chart said you are a law student. As a med student I lived in a crappy studio and ate cereal for dinner half the time."

He glanced out the window. The sky was wonderfully blue for New York City. "My parents, I suspect, are not like yours back in Minnesota. I was shot on their yacht, remember?"

Jennifer used her napkin to dab her mouth and nodded. "A very valid point. *I'm* even wondering why the hell I'm here."

She'd lost her mind.

Jennifer Ann Altea did not flirt with patients, she did not want an association with any sort of illegal activity, and quite frankly, she was not that fond of lawyers, especially those who got shot during some kind of elite cocktail party on an expensive boat.

But she *liked* him. And she did very much favor intelligent men. Salvatore Ariano was not just attractive but also had some sort of mysterious draw that she couldn't put her finger on. But everyone else on the planet—even his ex-girlfriend—seemed to notice she liked him. This had never happened to her before. Even though he was obviously a little not-with-it from the meds, he was still polite and genial and managed to be fairly charming.

Not an easy task.

There were no illusions: she was not a raving beauty, but she thought she was pretty in her own way, and he was interested in her too, she got that. But as she'd told him before, this was just an interesting situation. Why the hell couldn't she go for the insurance agent who'd accidentally run over his foot with a lawn mower last week? He'd been seriously coming on to her, even with two missing toes. And he was cute, but not like this guy. . . .

When Sal had been admitted, and sent into emergency surgery, the nurses had been talking about him from that first moment he was wheeled into the ED—she understood entirely why. Aside from his good looks, there was a certain charisma.

She should run the other way, but instead she propped her elbows on the table and asked him, "Why law school?"

His smile was disarming, and she was pleased to see he'd eaten his breakfast swiftly, which meant he was at least healing. Lack of appetite was a red flag. The food had done him good too, for his color was better.

He regarded her, across a table that she would guess cost thousands of dollars at the finest boutique antique store. The entire place was decorated with exquisite taste. He said readily enough, "My undergrad degree is in accounting and I got my CPA as soon as I graduated. I took a job with a firm, but it was a little boring for me, and my father encouraged me to go on to law school. I thought about it, and decided it wasn't a bad idea."

"So you could work in organized crime?"

His gaze was steady. "I immediately invoke a very famous amendment to the Constitution of the United States of America."

"Now you sound like a lawyer."

"That's promising. I certainly hope so." He leaned the elbow of his good arm on the table and took another sip of coffee. "So, this is not a one-way street. Why medical school?"

She brushed back her hair and contemplated her coffee cup. Then she slightly lifted her shoulders. "I don't really recall the conscious choice. I think I'd been inclined that direction all along. I loved biology and to be truthful, it is very interesting. That was my undergrad degree. Who else gets to work in a discipline where the variables are so vast that what works for one patient doesn't work at all for another? I never know what is going to happen from day to day and it is an adventure."

"That's how you look at it?"

"Pretty much. Long hours, very little thanks, and the money is okay but not what everyone thinks it is."

Sal touched his hand to the bandage on his side. "I have a certain appreciation for your dedication to your work."

"You have any idea who shot you?" Jennifer looked at him intently. "Like *none* of that was on television. I watched the next morning. Not a word. A man is shot on a yacht and no one mentions it? Impossible."

His face went shuttered. "My father has friends. High up."

"That I have gathered." She took a sip of coffee.

"No. Actually, *I* don't so much. You are judging me by the standards I don't necessarily hold."

Damn it, why was he so cute with those truly beautiful eyes? She didn't need this.

Her lashes lowered and she took in a breath. "You see, that could be a deal-breaker for me."

"We don't even have a deal yet, do we?"

Jennifer didn't laugh. Instead she spread her hands on the table. "I wish you were someone else."

"Oh man, that stings a bit." But he then added quietly, "I can't help it. It is what I am. I can give you some assurances. Principles vary. Don't believe everything you see on television. Every dime I will have in my lifetime will be earned by hard work. All of this life is a negotiation. CEOs of big companies regularly take golden parachutes and leave their employees bereft. No one calls them criminals. Except the people left wondering how they are going to make ends meet."

He had a point.

He went on. "I'm not condoning anything, either way. I'm just saying that life is gray, instead of black and white. I know how it sounds, but when you think about it, the law should be the law. In practice, that is not how it works. I can think of three very famous murder cases off the top of my head that when the defendant went to trial, everyone in this country knew they were guilty, but they got off because we couldn't prove it beyond the shadow of a doubt to that particular jury. It's a crapshoot, really."

That was pretty honest, and he was gorgeous with his bare chest—bandages aside—and his rumpled blond hair. He hadn't shaved, and she didn't mind that because it would certainly not be the easiest process to get out a razor and use it. For whatever reason, it made him seem less tall and dominant.

In her job, she got tired of arrogant males. Or females, for that matter. "I get what you are saying and I have not walked a mile in your shoes either." She picked up her coffee again. "Ethics are always a debatable topic. For instance, I should not have used your medical records to obtain your address."

"But yet I am glad you did. I think I'm glad in general you were the physician on duty. My lucky day."

He'd really been fortunate, and she was glad too.

No vital organs hit. A miracle. Maybe he had an idea of how much providence was involved, but from a medical point of view, he'd been a very lucky man. Taking a bullet to the stomach almost always involved greater damage.

Time for a change of subject. The kitchen was a dream, so that was a good place to start. She was trying to put a price tag on it and had no idea. Ceiling-to-floor cabinets with glass fronts and perfectly stacked expensive dishes, pendant lights in a sapphire blue glass, stainless steel appliances, and the view . . .

. . . water and the city skyline. Jennifer took another bite of her bagel. "I'm sitting here thinking that someday, I might live someplace like this. Of course I'm never home anyway, so it might be wasted on me. How do you afford it?"

Sal tried to shrug but winced instead. "I just lucked into it. My father knows the owner. Like I said, he knows people." He leaned forward. "I could use a roommate."

Jennifer had to be amused at his attempt to be seductive in his condition.

She wiped her fingers on her napkin. "First of all, you'd need to be completely lucid before you ask anyone that, and we haven't known each other long enough. Let's keep this all in perspective. I think you're attractive, but you have been on pain-killers since the first moment you woke up and looked into my eyes. Once life has achieved some sort of balance, maybe let's catch a movie, okay? I'm not certain a flirtation you will never remember is the basis of a relationship that involves sharing a sink."

"If you think I'd forget you, think again."

He looked visibly startled after he said it, like the remark had been involuntary, and maybe it had been.

"I meant—"

She took pity on him. "You aren't committing to anything or even scaring me away. Just relax. Middle ground here. A movie in our future?"

"Sure."

Jennifer leaned forward and touched his hand. Not the way she regularly touched her patients, but very differently. "I'm taking your friend's word for it and believing you are a nice guy. Now, let's take those bandages off to look at how you're healing and I will leave after that. I have a surgery at one o'clock anyway. It would be nice to get in a few hours of sleep."

After years of the clinic and supervising wound care, she had to admire how he didn't even move a muscle as she peeled off the dressing to inspect the wounds. He simply sat in the chair in that very stylish kitchen and let her do it, with the spectacular view of the Hudson River in the background, his jaw set tautly.

It had to hurt, but neither injury seemed infected, so the news was good. She wrapped and taped everything back up, and she just said mildly, "When you feel a little better, give me a call. Don't overdo it, okay?"

Then she leaned over and kissed him very lightly on the lips before she went out the door.

# TWENTY

T his is crazy pants."

Reign gazed at her assistant. "Louise, what are you talking about?"

"The clothing line . . . I can't get over it. I mean I was hoping. . . . I kept telling myself it would be you, but the competition is cutthroat in this business. Not to sound selfish, but this isn't just your big chance, it's mine too. I'll know a top designer. I'll have worked for her, with her, and when Reign Grazi becomes a household name, I'll hopefully be along for the ride."

The young woman paced around the small studio. It was definitely a spare space, part of an old factory with cinderblock walls and high windows, but it was practical and fairly cheap, and Reign's father owned the building.

Louise had elfin features: tip-tilted nose, eyes with a slight slant to them, and a small pointed chin. . . . And she was a wiz with a sewing machine. The best

Reign had ever seen, and even though Louise was just twenty-one, her enthusiasm and energy alone made Reign glad she'd hired her. No college, no experience except working in a clothing factory for a year, but she'd proven to be a good call. Reign didn't know much about her assistant's childhood, but she got the impression maybe there hadn't been a lot of money. Louise had mentioned once briefly that her mother had done alterations and mending to help make ends meet, in addition to her job as a waitress, and was one of the most tired people she'd ever known.

In amusement, Reign said, "I swear I think you are more excited than I am, and I am pretty wound up about the whole deal."

This morning Louise wore fishnet stockings, a short black skirt, and a lacy pink top with a black bra underneath. Clunky black heels completed the ensemble, and her hair was an unusual red not found in nature, at least not in most human beings.

But once again, she was really good at her job.

"Let's go over the first design again, can we?" Reign's desk was more of a disaster than usual, a computer angled at one end and her new sketches scattered everywhere. "I've picked out the fabrics and colors and I want to see how it works. Cocktail dress, my size, and let's make the skirt full, so more women feel comfortable wearing it. This will be a mass-market enterprise, not just for certain body types."

"Not all of us have your figure." Louise had wide hips, but a pretty petite bosom.

"Not everyone has my nose either," Reign pointed out wryly. "Supposedly it gives my face character."

"Men don't seem to mind."

She glanced up at the sound of the male voice and set aside her sketch pen as she realized someone was in the doorway. "Joey."

Louise audibly gasped, which was rather funny, but then again Joey Carre had an iconic name in the business that was more recognizable than Reign's. This afternoon he wore a flamboyant red shirt—that he actually looked good in—and dark gray slacks, leather Italian loafers, and his smile flashed white teeth.

"Reign." He strolled in, and she automatically rose to give him a swift kiss on the cheek. She hadn't seen him since he had introduced her to Nick at that party. It felt like it had been years.

He squeezed her shoulders. "Congratulations."

"Thanks." She sank back into her chair. "Nice of you to drop by. Have a seat. Do you want a cup of coffee or something?"

Louise rushed to pick a pile of magazines off a chair. "Espresso?"

"Thanks, sweetheart. Sounds wonderful." Joey sat, his smile benign, not even glancing over. "I've been coveting a breakthrough like yours for years, but that's hardly a secret because, let's face it, we all do. The New York fashion scene is buzzing over Reign Grazi."

Reign said dryly, "The New York fashion scene is always buzzing about something. I think you told me that the day I first met you."

"True, you're just the flavor of the hour, but savor it, Reign. Tell me, you still seeing Fattelli?"

"No secrets in this town, I take it." She lifted her shoulders. "Some, yes."

"Word is all the time."

The man in question was at the café across the street, working, but also, as Nick had pointed out, keeping an eye on the street and the doorway to her building. She said mildly, "I like Italian men."

Joey chuckled. "You like good-looking men, and he just happens to be Italian. Speaking of your ex, how's Vince? What's he up to?"

"On Long Island right now, having a little vacation with a family friend."

"Someone I know?"

"Probably." In an effort to change the subject, she pushed a piece of paper toward her unexpected guest. "Since you're here, what do you think of this design?"

The conversation then became centered on the cut of the neckline, and while Reign was the designer, she always respected someone else's opinion, or at least listened to it. Joey's taste might be a bit eclectic, but he was the tuning fork of the world she worked in. Style was an interesting facet to every personality. Not everyone liked the same thing, so that was just a stone cold fact. However, appealing to the most people possible was the important slant to every single career in her profession.

He sipped his drink and offered some pretty good advice, and when he left, she went right back to work.

An hour later, she took a break and called Sal. "How are you doing?"

"Well, still not able to leap buildings in a single bound, but I'm not sure I was ever up for that anyway, so maybe not all that disappointed."

"You sound good." She *did* care about him and felt a nostalgic sense of their lost romance. The good part was that their friendship was growing, even if it was entirely in a different direction. And, in her mind, everyone could always use another friend.

He told her, "Dr. Altea stopped by with breakfast and changed my bandages. If you weren't such an audacious bitch, that wouldn't have happened, so I guess I should thank you."

"Bitch? I've never been called that before." *Yeah, right.* About a thousand times by her ex-husband, which was part of the reason he was her ex-husband. She didn't mind the label as long as it wasn't said vindictively. "And yes, you should thank me. *You* wouldn't have made a move."

"Can those two bullet holes excuse me from my less than flirtatious behavior?"

"I like your shyness, but if I wasn't an audacious bitch you and I wouldn't have slept together either. I needed to step in."

"Reign." He laughed, and then it cut off and a second later he said on a suffocated voice, "Don't do that to me again, okay?"

"Fuck you? You seemed to like it—"

"Stop being funny."

She took mercy on him. "I'm sorry. I was just calling to see if you needed anything."

"I need *you,* but it isn't going to happen, is it?" He sounded wistful, but resigned.

Gently, she said, "No."

"Damn it, Reign. Why would you ever pick Fattelli over me?"

"Sal, I could never hurt him like I could hurt you." She looked out the window and tried to quell the pang of regret.

On the other end of the line, he blew out a breath she could clearly hear. "I hate to break it to you, but you've already hurt me."

"It was a compliment."

"And maybe you're selling *him* short. Ever think of that?"

This conversation was getting entirely too involved. Evidently he felt the same way, for he added, "Sorry. My fault. I keep bringing up the same topic when I already know the answer. Call me tomorrow?"

"I will." She ended the call and frowned at the latest sketch. This was going to be entirely different from anything she'd done before. Part of the deal was swimwear, and she was much more comfortable with evening wear and formal attire in general. It was a little difficult to make a bikini unique, but a challenge was a challenge.

An idea occurred to her and she started to work, putting a hint of a ruffle on the tiny skirt of the suit bottom, which she never did, but the cut of the suit would be perfect for it. Along with that, she decided on a deep purple for the color, which made her consider that later she might need a big chilled glass of wine because—purple, really? But it worked, and sometimes taking chances paid off. . . .

"You look pretty intent."

Reign glanced up. Nick leaned in the doorway of the studio, a faint smile on his face. "I'm at work," she informed him. "So I'm working."

"Is it okay if I use your restroom? I'm not a germ freak or anything, but I wanted to check in and I assume yours will be cleaner here than the one across the street."

"Right there." Louise pointed at the door. "Like right there."

"Thanks."

As soon as he went in and the latch clicked shut, she leaned a hand on Reign's desk. "Who the fuck is that? Seriously? First Joey Carre—*the* Joey Carre—and now this guy? Checking in? Why?"

"He's a . . . friend."

"With benefits, I'm guessing." Louise tilted her head back with an exaggerated sigh. "I have *friends* and none of them look like him. . . . He's gorgeous. His shirt cost more than a new set of tires on my car and he wears it well. Have you thought about using him as a model?"

Reign took a moment to contemplate how that suggestion might go over and stifled a laugh. "I don't think he likes being photographed. Besides, he's an investment banker. I'd guess he doesn't need whatever we could pay him."

A loose description. Maybe Nick was a little bit more than an investment banker, but keep it simple.

Louise wasn't buying it. She had some pretty discerning street smarts. "My ass that's all he is."

Reign took in a breath. "He's a very beautiful man. I agree with that. What else he might be I don't know, and maybe we should not push to find out. Get it?"

"Of course I would model."

It was always fun toying with Reign and this was no exception. She turned and sent him a glare that would incinerate the devil.

To ashes. In the depths of hell.

He liked her office. It was business-like, and though he would have never chosen the red-and-white-striped chair she sat in, it worked. There were shelves and filing cabinets, and her desk held the usual clutter of a laptop, pens, and a stack of business cards, but it was definitely an organized mess. He also liked her in a soft pink blouse and a casual skirt, because he was used to seeing her dressed up, or entirely undressed. Both were great, but this was nice too.

"You were listening?" Her nape looked soft and tempting under a very business-like upsweep of ebony hair secured by a gold clip.

"I walked out of the bathroom and heard you," he said with no hint of defensiveness. "Am I supposed to apologize?"

At least she owned it. "No. I just assumed you'd politely pretend you didn't hear."

"I didn't know you also designed men's clothing."

"There is a lot about me you don't know."

*Don't count on it, sweetheart.*

Louise chimed in. "Don't assume anything about Reign. She designed that chair she's sitting in. Awesome, isn't it?"

Nick rested a hip on her desk and crossed his arms over his chest. "She's *very* talented. I can attest to that."

"She isn't referring to blow jobs, darling." Reign said it with false sweetness, leaning back in her chair and twirling a pen between her fingers.

"You have a younger brother? I give good blow jobs." The rather eccentric young woman who appeared to be an assistant or secretary was obviously enjoying the exchange, her mouth twitching into a gamine smile.

"Sorry, honey, his brother's a priest," Reign informed her. "Will you excuse us for a second? Maybe go get us lunch? I was thinking Chinese."

The young woman left, muttering, "A priest, that's practically a crime."

When the door closed, Reign said quietly, "She was joking. She's a nice girl."

He spread his hands. "You happen to be the one who brought up blow jobs. I merely gave you a compliment. What did Carre want?"

"Just to say congratulations." She tilted her head toward the window that faced the street and the café where he'd been all morning. "Everything quiet down there while you were buying and selling stocks and probably making millions?"

"So far, so good."

He hadn't seen anything suspicious, which was somewhat of a relief, but he couldn't quite get past the idea that he might be missing something crucial. It bothered him.

"Want to work in here instead?" Her face held a troubled expression when she turned back. "I don't like you sitting there exposed at a table on a busy thoroughfare. Anyone could take a shot."

"Are you protecting me?"

"Is there an objection?"

"No."

He leaned forward and let his mouth linger inches from hers. "You sure?"

She wanted to kiss him. He could tell.

"Oh, Fattelli, just go back to the café."

"I thought you just invited me to stay." He straightened, still propped on her desk.

She laid her hand on his thigh and her green eyes were somber. "It isn't like I care or anything, but maybe you *should* stay."

He was starting to realize that her armor was penetrable, but he really needed to be the right man. Decision time for *him*, just as much as for her.

It was comical, when he considered it. Covering her hand with his and entwining their fingers, he was pretty much as afraid of this as he sensed she was.

Maybe more.

And he was never afraid.

"You don't care about me?" He asked it softly.

She glanced away at the window. The view of the

cars going by was about the same, the street busy, the apartment building above the café baked by the sun. "Maybe I didn't say that the right way. 'Care' implies something I don't want to imply, and you don't want to hear, so—"

"Hey, that's the second time this afternoon you've decided what I do or do not want. Speaking of which, I keep in shape, so let me model something. I might not be twenty-five or anything, but I might be useful. Don't overlook the possibilities right in front of you."

"Really? You're serious?" It was Reign's turn to cross her arms in front her chest, freeing her hand first. "Down a catwalk, jacket flung over your shoulder?"

"I might." His smile crinkled the corner of his eyes.

"You might even like it. You might not be twenty-five, but you know how you look. All the women would be drooling on themselves. Uhm, no. Rule one: I don't share. That happens to be *my* dick unless you choose to put it somewhere else, in which case, it is all yours again."

She wasn't so much difficult to understand—he had some personal issues himself—as she was hard to handle. Their relationship was starting to make her wary, and he was wary as hell too, and . . . where was this going?

"Your ex-husband cheated?" He asked it cautiously.

"My ex-husband did almost everything possible wrong." Her eyes were like glittering green diamonds, but then she softened. "Except I do think he loves his son. He just doesn't understand how to do it the right way, and I'm sorry, as hard as I tried, I couldn't teach him. That's a path he's going to have to figure out for himself if he ever makes the effort. It'll be fine. Vince knows we both love him. He's very bright. He *gets* it. I've got to say he's one kid that knows the tension is between his father and me and not anything really to do with him. He's never blamed himself like some kids of divorced parents."

Nick reached out and did what he'd been wanting to do since he walked in, which was loosen the clip in her raven hair. It spilled over her shoulders in an inky fall.

"Nicky," she said in reproof, trying to gather it up, the action lifting her breasts in an enticing fashion. "What are you doing?"

"Yes, Nicky," a voice said, silky smooth. "What *are* you doing?"

# TWENTY-ONE

Reign turned her head and stared at the woman
standing in the doorway.
   She recognized her from the night on the
yacht when Sal was shot. Blond, very pretty, her
make up done perfectly, and wearing a green dress
definitely not off the rack.

*Why the hell is she here?*

Nick looked just as startled. He cast Reign an
inquiring glance and moved casually to block any
direct view. Luckily he had very nice wide shoulders. Pleasantly, he said, "I think we met before on
the Arianos' yacht."

"I'm Carmen."

"Right."

She sauntered in and glanced around at the cin-
der block walls, the spools of fabric resting against
them, and the factory window, and said, "I kind of
expected more, you know? This big designer thing,
so I'd have expected something really chic, ya know.

But I'm not all that impressed. I'm not getting it." The words were slightly slurred.

What Reign didn't get was what the visit might be about. She edged a view around Nick's shoulder. "Sorry to disappoint. We work here."

She suddenly understood Nick's protective stance. The woman was carrying a gun casually in her hand. Reign's entire body chilled.

*Okay. Easy.*

Sal had mentioned her before. Reign knew her family, but she was quite a bit younger, not *that* much older than Vince, and they'd never been introduced. This was beyond awkward and into some zone she'd never visited before.

Nick moved again to obstruct her view, and apparently use his body as a shield, so she no longer had any grasp on the situation. "I'm not sure what you thought you might see." His voice was utterly calm. "First time I've been here too, but like you it just seems like an office to me. But then again, like she said, people do work here."

Reign whispered, "She's obsessed with Sal."

Sal had mentioned once that Carmen texted him so often it had started to make him uncomfortable, and that even as a teenager she'd been pretty sexually aggressive.

Nick said quietly, "I'm getting there is something going on. I have never hurt a woman, so this could get interesting, but if she swings that weapon our way, all bets are off. I'll take her down."

"Why are you whispering?" Carmen turned from inspecting a bolt of scarlet silk that was pooled on the floor. Her eyes were visibly dilated, even from a distance, and Reign got the first jolt that told her maybe something besides Sal was a part of this impromptu visit.

Drugs. *Great. Perfect.*

"What do you want?" Nick asked it casually, like he was inquiring if she wanted some iced tea.

"Just to talk to Reign. You're in the way."

Reign couldn't even remember being quite so cold. She'd been shot at enough lately. This was becoming surreal. Nick merely asked, "Why?"

"Sal and I. It won't happen while she's in the picture. I'm being practical." Carmen's sandals scraped the floor, but Reign couldn't see what she was doing. "Tell me, why do *you* like her so much, Mr. Fattelli? Or should I call you Nicky like she does?"

He said gently, "I think you might be a little under the influence"

"Of?"

"I'm not quite sure. Apparently it is a substance that makes you think it is acceptable to walk into a design business carrying a gun before lunch and threaten the owner. Sort of like robbing a convenience store, but with a little more class. You do realize the weapon you have pointing my direction is much more likely to take out a window if you fire it? You can't even hold it steady."

"Are you sure?" Carmen sounded a little less hostile and more confused.

Maybe time to do something to help as well. Someone else might have wanted to call 911, but she wasn't that person. Reign took out her phone and pushed a different button. When Sal answered she said, "Carmen is here. Maybe you could call her parents."

"Oh shit." His voice was thick. "I was asleep. . . . Yeah, give me a minute to wake up . . . these pain-killers. *Why* exactly is she there?"

"I'm not sure, but she has a gun and I think it has something to do with you."

"Reign. *Shit*." He obviously woke up.

"Nick is here too and it is fairly under control. . . . But call them? She seems pretty high and really wants to point that gun at me, but at the moment, Nick gets that honor."

She could hear Nick talking in the background in that same even voice, and Carmen was respond-ing, but with him between them Reign wasn't quite sure what was happening. She was only barely able to hear him since her heart was pounding so hard the beat echoed in her ears.

Sal said, "Are you fucking kidding me? I'll be right there."

"No." Reign kept her voice low. "First of all, you are in no shape to drive and we both know it. Maybe just talk to her a little?" She tapped Nick on the shoulder. "Would you mind handing her my phone? It's Sal."

"I'll set your phone on the edge of the desk, but she'll have to come get it." He reached behind with an open palm but didn't as much as look anywhere except, apparently, at Carmen, who Reign couldn't really see. He leaned forward and then straightened again. "Sal wants to talk to you. Maybe you could set down the gun when you pick up the phone."

"How do I know that's Sal?" she asked suspiciously. "You're trying to trick me."

"I don't try and trick anyone. Since you know my name, maybe you know my reputation. Tricks just aren't my thing. By the way, your father is a pretty no-nonsense kind of man. He isn't going to be happy with you over this little stunt. Now, just set down the gun and talk to Sal. No harm, no foul, Carmen."

"He's only interested in *her*." There was a definite wobble of tears in her voice. "I don't even *want* to talk to him."

"If you don't pick it up and at least give him a chance, the other option is the police and they are going to bust you not just for attempted assault and possibly even attempted murder, but for taking whatever it is that has you thinking this was a viable option. If you drove here, and I sure am hoping you didn't, they'll get you for DUI too. Jail time isn't fun. I visited way too many people in prison. None of them seem very happy with the situation."

To his credit, the man was persuasive and utterly unruffled. Reign had to give him that. A moment later, he moved with lightning speed, and she saw he was in possession of the gun and Carmen had her phone, and she was speaking incoherently into it, tears running down her pale face.

Louise chose that moment to walk back in, her hands full of paper bags. She stopped short, taking in the sobbing woman on the phone and Nick holding the gun. Eyes wide, she said, "Holy crap, a girl steps out for two seconds to grab some Chinese food and she misses everything."

"Well, I will say Reign Grazi is never boring." Nick held the door for Reign later that afternoon and watched as she gracefully kicked off her shoes and sank down on the couch in their hotel suite.

Reign shut her eyes. "I suppose that's something."

"Can I make her a cocktail?"

"You know my tipple."

"Yes I do. Pink and delicious. Fits perfectly into my mouth." He grinned and moved toward the bar.

"I didn't say 'nipple.'" She opened one eye. A good sign. She did seem a little wiped out. Who could blame her? If he hadn't happened to be there, it could have gone south pretty fast. He wasn't giving himself the credit for a fairly amicable resolution, but unfortunately it could easily have been tragic. Reign wasn't the type to call for assistance, so who knows what might have happened.

He murmured, "Oh, my mistake. The usual?"

"Of course." She sat up. "Do you think that maybe all this time, Carmen has been the one? Maybe she's the one who hired the man you shot in my closet."

He reached up and took a bottle off the top shelf, carefully poured two fingers of Johnnie Walker Black into a glass, and added ice from the drawer. "No."

She didn't either, he could tell as he walked around to hand the glass to her. Reign at least offered a faint smile. "It would be nice if it was that easy, right?"

"She's just a little messed up." Nick settled down next to her. For himself he'd grabbed a cold Corona, and he took a drink. "Sal Ariano doesn't do too much for me, but it seems he did at one time for you, and she sure seems like she's into the idea of a relationship with him."

"*He'd* like to know what I see in you that I don't see in him." Reign propped her now bare feet on the coffee table.

"My charm, I suppose."

She stared at her bare toes, which were nicely tinted with pink polish. "As I haven't quite figured it out yet myself, I avoided that answer."

"No comment, but I doubt if she hired them they would have accidentally shot Salvatore Ariano unless they are completely inept."

No, they'd merely shot the tall man standing next to Reign Grazi.

Him. Seconds after Sal had come over to talk to her, but they'd thought it was him.

It was hard to deny he might have been the target that night, but she'd definitely been the goal this afternoon. He also understood why. She looked delectable in the soft blouse, her hair tumbling everywhere.

Ariano was in love with her.

And so was he.

It stopped Nick as he sat there, like a moment

frozen in time. That wasn't why he'd stepped between Reign and Carmen's murderous tendencies this afternoon. . . . He would have done that for quite a few people, and truly, he'd felt in charge of the situation once he'd known what was going on.

It wasn't even why he'd insisted she stay with him, and it wasn't really anything about their relationship, except he liked her there next to him. Not just because he desired her—he did, but that was a little different.

It felt like the right fit. She was fiery and sexy and brave, but also compassionate and caring in many ways.

Her sense of independence was something they had in common. He'd had his since his father was killed, so on that level, they really understood each other. Right now he was protecting her, but never would she ask him to take care of her. That was not Reign and it never would be, and he understood it.

Simple, but true.

He *loved* her.

*Oh shit.* This was going to freak her out, because he wasn't about to give her up to Ariano or anyone else, yet she didn't want a man involved in her life in a permanent way. He hadn't even met her son yet, but he wanted to, which was a first in his life.

"Nicky?"

He realized she was looking at him expectantly. "What did you just say?"

Her brows drew together. "I said that it was nice of Sal to meet them at the hospital when her parents decided to take Carmen in. He called me when

I was on my way here. That pretty doctor came and picked him up and took him to the Emergency Department, since Carmen was incoherent and they thought seeing him might calm her down until they figured out what she was on."

"What was it?"

"Cocaine, I take it, or that's what she *thought* it was. A couple of the friends she was sharing that particular recreational experience with had a similar bizarre reaction. She's doing pretty well, or that's what he said. They don't think it was very pure, but when dealing with people who sell drugs, who can you trust?"

"Very few. She picked the wrong dealer." Nick reached over and took her feet and swung them onto his lap. "Lie back and relax. That's decent of Ariano to go there and decent of you to feel sorry for her, all things considered."

"You don't like Sal?"

"Of course not, Reign."

A true look of confusion crossed her features. "He's—"

"Frickin' nice. I know. I've heard about it often enough. Don't worry, the feeling is mutual. He hates my guts because we're involved. I don't like him because he's slept with you and it's pretty obvious he misses the event."

"*He* suggested I stay with you."

"Because he would rather see me take a bullet than you and knows I'd do it. That doesn't mean he likes me. It means he likes you." Nick rubbed her foot, sensuously massaging the arch. "Look, I don't care what his motivations are or even how he feels, though obviously you do, but he has the right idea. I suppose I am going to grudgingly admit today was not his fault, but still, you need me."

"Who are you trying to convince? Me or you?" Reign reclined against the cushions and her gaze was steady. "And while you think over the answer, please keep rubbing my feet because that feels really, really good."

"I think I've made up *my* mind."

"That I need you?"

"Or I need you. Could be a two-way street."

"I drove down a street I thought was two-way before. Turned out to be a dead end."

"Hey, don't lump us all in together."

"Sorry, but in my experience, most men think with their dicks."

"That is an undeniable truth." He smiled wickedly on purpose and trailed his hand up her thigh. "Guess what mine is thinking right now?"

"The usual." She sipped her drink. "You're kind of predictable, Fattelli."

"I like a woman who understands me." To his disappointment, he discovered she was wearing underwear, but on the bright side, that could always be removed.

Reign gave him a considering look. "Knowing you can't wait to get me into bed does not mean I understand you. With your hand up under my skirt, I'm not going to take a lot of credit for that obvious conclusion. To say I understand you is an assumption I don't think I agree with at all."

Considering the revelation he was still grappling with from a few moments ago, he had no desire to have her know what he was thinking. Instead he leaned forward and kissed her. She tasted like fine whisky and Reign, which happened to be a very fine combination. Against her lips he murmured, "You were absolutely right. I can't wait to get you into my bed."

# TWENTY-TWO

Mind telling me the story?"

God, he hated hospitals, especially considering his recent stay. Sal accepted the cup of coffee with a murmured thank you. He shook his head. "There isn't one really. Carmen and I have known each other most of our lives. Small world and all. Thanks for picking me up, by the way."

And more so for bringing him home.

Dr. Altea looked quite different in street clothes once again. She wore slacks and a sleeveless white blouse and held her coffee cup in two hands. They were on the small tiled terrace off his condo and the evening was pretty pleasant. There were two chairs and a glass table out there, but he almost never used it.

She frowned. "I was actually halfway home when they called me. It happens all the time. The ED doctor recognized your name and knew I'd been your physician. Your friend was in a pretty deep downward spiral when she was admitted."

He considered the clematis climbing up a trellis on the brick wall that separated the small backyard from that of his neighbor. The purple blooms were delicate and perfect, but that was hardly due to his diligent care. Sal said in a subdued voice, "Carmen is not a drug addict in my opinion, just unlucky today."

"Have you had unprotected intercourse with her?"

He shot her a direct look. His side hurt. His shoulder hurt. "Drop the doctor thing. No sex with her at all and thanks for the personal inquiry."

Jennifer looked pragmatic. "I'm fairly jaded when it comes to patients that come in who use drugs. Not only is their judgment in general impaired, but it isn't like the FDA regulates what they choose to put into their bodies. There's a reason it is illegal. If you had slept with her, you should be tested, that's all."

It was true, he'd almost had sex with Carmen the night he was shot, but he wouldn't be so stupid as to have unprotected sex with anyone he didn't know, or even her. "I don't think she's like that."

"Under the influence, people make really bad decisions, like wanting to kill your ex-girlfriend Ms. Grazi."

The sky had deepened enough that stars were scattered about and visible despite the city lights. Sal looked up at the velvet sky and mused. "Reign was never really my girlfriend. Friend, yes, and still one, but I expected more than she wanted to give, so end of story. We were involved, but calling it more than that is really pushing it. Neither did Carmen have any right to go off the deep end and be jealous. I've promised her nothing."

"And never will?"

"Never will."

"That's pretty blunt. She's quite a pretty young woman."

He looked at Jennifer, registered the self-confidence she projected, and shook his head. "I don't want pretty. Let me rephrase," he said hastily as her brows rose. "I don't want *just* pretty. I want interesting. I want someone who can make their own way, and maybe would like someone to share their life down the line but not necessarily count on me to solve every problem."

"Very diplomatic, Counselor."

He muttered, "Good to hear, since I'm hardly at my best."

"I think you can be excused under the circumstances." Dr. Altea's topaz eyes were very direct as usual, and he had to wonder just what had prompted her to turn her car around and head toward his address when she could have ignored the whole debacle. "Want to know what I'm looking for?"

He reclined his head back and shut his eyes. "Someone who doesn't get shot or have friends brandishing weapons at other friends? Just a guess. May I note I was about to say 'this is just a shot in the dark,' but that would be the worst comment possible."

She choked on her coffee, laughing. "I want a guy who is attractive, has tons of deadly friends, and seems to lead quite an interesting life all around. I might throw in a nice sense of humor, compassion, and of course, would defend me pro bono in court should a malpractice suit ever come up."

Sal opened his eyes. "I might know someone like that. But I don't know if he does pro bono work. He might require some passionate sex in return. Just a warning."

In a serene voice, she said, "Maybe payment could be arranged on a case-by-case basis. In the meantime, let's admire the stars, finish our coffee, and I'll be on my way."

That sounded like a perfect plan. If he could sweep her up in his arms, carry her to the bed—which would normally be possible since he was considerably larger as a human being—he would, but that wasn't happening.

At least not tonight.

So he settled for saying, "Would it be wrong of him to ask for a retainer . . . like next week?"

"Isn't he being a little optimistic?" Jennifer Altea lifted her brows, relaxed in her chair.

"Oh, I think he'll be more than capable."

"What if that isn't what I meant?"

That drew a grin, and a teasing tone he was surprised he could summon to the inquiry. "I guess we'll find out next week, right?"

It was not the sort of thing she'd normally do.

Reign paused in front of the church, wishing she

could have managed some different sort of venue. It was a beautiful stone building, and old, with a slight hint of lichen climbing up the foundation, and it had a small bronze sign posted by the doors into the vestibule that said it had been established in 1855.

As she went up the steps, she wondered if she was doing the right thing at all.

But she had to admit that the day before had taught her an interesting lesson. She'd taken for granted that the blonde who had such a thing for Sal was just a young woman with a crush.

That hadn't gone so well, and it could have been much worse for both of them. Her father had always told her she underestimated or overestimated people and needed to find some middle ground.

*Definitely underestimated this time.*

The church had an undefinable smell that only existed in old buildings like this one, choir robes and a thousand spent candles and pews that were slowly going to dust. Reign walked past a few people who were leaving the building and then was consumed by the silence as she entered the sanctuary. Beautiful windows and a soaring ceiling held her attention, the altar raised, the aisle carpet soft under her feet.

There was a nun who smiled at her as she passed, and she asked in a hushed voice, "Father Fattelli?"

"Go through that door, child." The woman pointed. "He was in his office just a few moments ago. I'd guess he's still there."

So priests had offices? How odd. She'd really

not thought about that before, but as Reign followed the directions, she imagined they must. It was, in essence, a job after all.

Well, a calling more than a job, but . . .

The man she met in the hallway was so like Nick she stopped short and stared. All that luscious dark hair and those striking blue eyes, but he wore a holy collar and smiled in an entirely different way. "Hello."

It took her a second to respond. "I'm . . . I'm Reign," she stammered. "Uhm, Reign Grazi. Can I talk to you for a minute? It isn't much of a guess to think you are just the person I came to see."

"I'm going to . . ." he started to say, but then nodded as if he sensed her unrest. "Of course. This way."

Louise would *definitely* be disappointed that this man had chosen a different path.

His office was plain and utilitarian, and he settled behind the desk after offering her a wooden chair. She was never uncomfortable around men—or women either, for that matter—but in this setting, she found it a little difficult to relax. Reign took in a breath and said plainly, "I am a very good friend of your brother."

"Well, let's see. Great legs and all that gorgeous hair. I'm not all that surprised. He's always had good taste." John Fattelli sounded very matter-of-fact. "Nick is usually very private. I'm surprised you even know I exist. We are brothers but do not have the same life. What brings you here, Ms. Grazi?"

"I think someone is trying pretty hard to kill him."

The response wasn't immediate, but eventually

it happened. "I've always been afraid of this." John Fattelli looked briefly away, his profile remote. When he looked back, he said in measured tones, "Tell me what brought you here."

She did. All of it. The man in the closet of her bedroom. Sal being shot on the yacht and how Nick had been standing there just minutes before. She tossed in the incident with Carmen, though she thought that had nothing to do with it.

Silence.

There was a clock on the wall that ticked loudly, but otherwise Nick's brother seemed to just be thinking about what she'd told him.

He finally took in a deep breath. "Has he told you about Catherine?"

"No." The chair could have been the most uncomfortable one she'd ever sat in, but Reign didn't even care. "He kind of talks around his past."

"Our sister. She married young, but a lot of Sicilian women do that. Her husband was abusive, and when she was pregnant with her first child, he hit her a bit too hard one evening. She fell and the blow to her head killed her. Her husband claimed she stumbled, but she'd just confided in our mother what was going on so we doubted that story, trust me. Unfortunately, though he was arrested initially on two counts of assault and manslaughter, there wasn't enough evidence to take it to trial, just our word for it he'd pushed her before."

John looked at his hands. "They were fraternal twins, so Nick really took it hard. We all did, but not like he did. He was a friend of her husband and introduced them. He won't talk about it. Flat out. I've tried. He just . . . won't."

The words actually explained quite a lot. Reign felt paralyzed, her throat tight.

He added, "We all deal with grief in our way. I became a priest, and he became something else entirely. I want to leave vengeance to the God I believe exists, and he wanted to make sure it happened while he was on this earth. Ms. Grazi, I can't even tell you which one of us is right, but I assure you that my sister's husband disappeared the day after he was released from jail, and while I am a man of the church, I will never ask about what happened to him, and neither do I care. But I bet Nick knows. My brother-in-law's parents were quite vocal in their accusations, but once again, nothing could be proven. Clever of my brother, an eye for an eye, I suppose. I think the justice of the Lord is meted out by various means, don't you? We all are instruments in his purpose."

Piety aside, he still hadn't answered her question. "Do you have any idea who might want him dead?"

"It would not surprise me if Nick had any number of enemies who might have murderous inclinations, but please understand we strictly do not discuss anything except baseball and occasionally he gives me investment advice. I'd like to think we're close but acknowledge we are two very different people. Morality is a sliding scale depending on the circumstances. For instance, I doubt any woman becomes a prostitute because she wants to, but they are judged very harshly. Marriage is a sacred vow, but my sister certainly should have broken it. My father was a dangerous man, but once I was old enough to realize what he did for a living, he told me that he never took a job if he didn't think the world would be a better place without that person."

"Nick was hired to kill me, but it was a setup."

John laughed softly. "Nick would never kill a beautiful woman like you. Besides, just from our brief conversation, and I consider myself a fairly wise judge of people, I don't at all think the world would be a better place without you. Quite the contrary, Ms. Grazi. Who would think so? I can't really imagine you having enemies that determined."

She thought about Carmen and had to admit she hadn't seen that one coming. Who would hate her? No one she could think of, but her family did have rivals.

It hit her then, like the proverbial lightning bolt, or considering her location, maybe a gift from above.

Rivals. Aggression and revenge could exist for many reasons, most of it based on either money or prestige.

Or maybe both.

She grabbed her purse and rose to stick out her hand. "I need to talk to Nick. It's been very . . . enlightening to meet you, Father. I suppose that's what I should call you, right?"

Nick's brother looked a little bewildered, but graciously shook her hand. "I think John would be fine."

When she stepped onto the sidewalk, her phone rang. She answered immediately. "Vince?"

Her son replied in a strained voice. "Hi. Mom. I wanted to let you know we're back in the city. Max's dad thought maybe it would be best. Hey, can you come pick me up?"

Whphone rang he was frowning at his computer screen, distracted, wondering why the hell he'd agreed to let Reign go anywhere alone, though she'd insisted she'd take the subway and then a cab, and no one would ever guess where she was going, and it was a safe place.

Nick saw the number with relief. "Where are you? I'm sitting in your office, unable to work. Never again, until we get this resolved, will I let you persuade me to let *you* go somewhere alone."

"You really liked my method of persuasion."

He had. A mind-blowing blow job first thing in the morning, followed by slow, steamy sex that involved enough heat he was tangled in the damp sheets afterward, and in a weak moment, he let her have her way.

She'd sworn it was an innocent errand.

"I've been worried."

She said urgently, "Meet me somewhere. We need

to talk, and don't say the location. My office could be bugged."

"Can you be more specific on where?" *And why does she suddenly think her office could be bugged?*

She texted him the location of an office building on 27th Street, and he was a little puzzled but more than happy to comply. He'd gotten nothing done all morning. He took a cab, since he couldn't be sure about the Bentley unless Pat swept it again, and parking was impossible anyway.

Reign was in the lobby, pacing a little, and it was nice to see her welcoming smile and the tension in her shoulders ease.

"Nicky." She came over and gave him a swift hug, but though he would have preferred she linger in his arms, she withdrew and pointed at a bench. "Shall we talk for a minute? I think you'll find what I have to say interesting."

Fake potted plants and tiled floors, he noted, but nice, with a receptionist and soft music in the background. "Where are we?"

"I have no idea. I just told the cab driver to stop. Nice, huh?" She looked at him intently with those notable green eyes as she sank down. "Answer a question for me, okay? How do you know Joey Carre?"

Carre? He'd met the man when he first came to New York at some social gatherings. Rich, successful designer, so it made sense he knew Reign. After all, it was Carre who had introduced them. "Through mutual friends. Why?"

Today she had her hair up again in some kind of

an elegant twist, but with a few ebony wisps framing her oval face. She licked her lips as if maybe her mouth was a little dry. "Tell me this: Who at that party when we first met could predict we might go home together? Think about it."

She had a point. Carre had homed in on the way Nick had been looking at her. In fact, he'd been the one to make sure they were left alone. "I am thinking about it," he said grimly. "He might, I suppose, be the best candidate."

"That man in my closet . . . he could have shot me, and then you, but he already knew you were probably armed, so he went for you first, right?"

"He knew I was armed because he tried to hire me to kill you." He said it slowly, casting back, thinking. "But I get where you're going. He was there before us and waiting, and he sure as hell was not invited to that fancy party. . . . So you think Carre tipped him off. Why?"

"Professional jealousy."

He had to admit, he hadn't thought of that. "The new clothing line? He's wealthy already, right?"

Reign nodded, her soft mouth pressed into a tight line. "Oh, he is. But I'm wondering if he coveted the job I just got for the prestige, which it does offer, more than the money. There's a chance I could become a pretty big name in the fashion world. Don't get me wrong, he's already pretty well known, but the competition for this one was tough."

Nick reached over and squeezed her hand lightly. "And he knew who the real competition was. I get it. You won. Why shoot Sal?"

Her eyes filled with tears. "I think he knew that might hurt me, but, in truth, they could have still been aiming for you. I don't know what happened that night. Maybe they just missed me like we first assumed."

"Friends are often enough jealous of other friends."

"You say that as if you know what it is like to be betrayed like this."

Nick looked at her and knew. Even with the bustle of the busy lobby and the ding of the elevator, he knew. "John, right? That's where you had to go so urgently this morning without me. I should never have mentioned he even existed."

It was possible he might have turned away and walked out—but she touched his arm. "Is it wrong I want to understand you? Where do you get off, Fattelli?"

There were tears on her cheeks and he wanted to kiss them away and make her happy.

Maybe it was just him, but he had the impression she very rarely cried. Some women did it for effect, and some to manipulate, but that wasn't her style. Real tears.

Wait a minute. *Oh fuck.*

"He told you about Catherine. Shit. Please, Reign, do me a favor and let's not discuss it, okay? John is far too much into wanting to talk, when action should just be taken. He and I couldn't be more different." He swiped away a tear from the corner of her eye with the tip of his finger.

"Funny, he said the exact same thing, so maybe not *that* much different." Her voice wobbled just a little.

"He's a *priest*."

"You sure aren't, but I get what you're saying. Joey went after my son, Nick."

He had a heartbeat moment in which he knew whatever he might say would not be the right thing, and then he let out a slow breath. "Tell me."

She explained. "I'm not saying it was a state secret or anything, but I *know* Joey knew Vince was with a friend on Long Island because I told him myself. Someone intercepted Vince and his friend coming back from the beach. Tried to sell him some story about an accident I was involved in, and I am happy to say my son is smart as hell, didn't like how the guy acted, and they both took off." Reign rubbed her forehead. "This is my fault."

"How the hell do you figure that? By being a better designer? Get real. Not your fault at all. Carre's fault. Would you have gone after him if he'd gotten the job instead? No."

"Okay." Her voice was stronger, wobble gone now, tears drying up. That was much more comfortable for him. "Point taken."

Nick looked around, but the lobby was still quiet, everyone innocuous and going about their business. "We need to draw him out. If it is Carre, what are the odds he'll back away?"

"I thought I knew him better than you do, but apparently not." Reign sniffled once more but her composure was back in place. She shook her head. "He won't run away. Not his style. If what has happened so far is him, he'll just fling it back in our face and dare us to prove it. We won't be able to, either. The fashion industry is ruthless and he's pretty much an endurable commodity. He isn't dumb, and all we have is my accusation he's behind it."

Nick sat for a minute. Once before, all he had was an instinct and he'd been dead right. A sick punch-to-the-gut feeling that his brother-in-law was the son of a bitch who had killed his sister. It hadn't taken but about two minutes for that bastard to confess he'd shoved her hard because they'd been arguing, once there was a gun involved in the situation.

Not an excuse—and Nick's father would have agreed, but he wasn't there to protect her—to touch a woman or a child in anger. The act of a coward. Nick might have been too late, but at least that fucker hadn't walked free.

No one would ever find *that* body. He had no regrets, no apologies to make, but he still lost a sister and he missed her every single day—though at least she was avenged. It wasn't enough, but it was something.

Catherine had been so delighted about the baby. She'd told him before she'd even told that asshole of a husband . . . and Nick had been happy for her also. Life was just sometimes plain cruel, but there were checks and balances.

Reign was not going to be part of the conversation he had with Joey Carre.

"Call Ariano," he said, and it was reluctant, but necessary. "Let me sort this out with Carre. Go stay with Sal."

"Jesus, who are the two of you, ordering me around? He wants me to stay with you, now you want me to stay with him—"

He interrupted. "Reign, lower your voice, and while you do that, think about it. I want you with me, and he wants you with him. We both have a common goal of keeping you safe, however, so we are giving in on several levels of male negotiation that maybe you can't quite understand. But get that it's not easy for us. Call him."

Reign wasn't exactly effusive. She looked great in something black and white she'd undoubtedly designed herself, but Sal's attention wasn't really on her clothes even though the tailored skirt did nice things for her legs. "What's this about?'

She dropped on his couch and the set of her mouth indicated she was tired. "I hope you are going to offer me a glass of wine before I explain."

He glanced at the clock. "A merlot?"

"Chardonnay, if you have it. A merlot will need to breathe and I don't want to wait. Hold on a minute." She seemed to come into the moment and got to her feet. "You don't need to wait on me. I'm sorry. Stay where you are. I'll find it. Sal, don't you dare move. You're hardly even close to recovered."

"I'm not an invalid and I do think there's a bottle in the refrigerator."

"*Don't* move." It amused him when she got militant.

"I might dare."

She shot him a look. "You'll be sorry."

"Will I?" They were sitting in his living room, and with appreciation he watched her retrieve the corkscrew from the drawer in the kitchen and rummage around for the wine. In a few minutes she brought him a glass as well.

When she sat back down she said, "Ever since this started, Nick and I have been going back and forth, wondering what's happening. Is it him? Is it me? Carmen didn't help either—that was *you*—but you've been hurt too."

"But if he dropped you off here, he must have some sort of agenda." Sal liked the wine; it was smooth and mellow and he had sworn off the pain meds, so he liked it even more, but that was hardly the point.

"Joey Carre." She said it in a low voice. "Fuck, why didn't I think of it before? He knows you, he knows me, and he knows Nicky. He's a designer, and he's very competitive and knows the Life. I got that offer. He didn't. He's pissed. He saw it coming and tried to narrow the playing field. He even came to my office to congratulate me and pointed out he'd been waiting his whole career for what just landed in my lap. He's threatened my son, and you know, I just can't take that."

It made sense. A little too much.

"Reign," he said carefully, setting aside the glass. "Do you have any idea how dangerous Carre is? He seems pretty harmless, right? Silk suits, narrow ties, and a white smile, but he's a bull shark. Great whites get all the press, but bull sharks bite more people. Not the worst that can happen to you, but much more likely to strike. Does Fattelli understand this?"

"How am I supposed to answer that?" Her green eyes were filled with dismay. "I think so. He said I needed to come here and stay with you and to be sure you were armed. Joey Carre? He's like . . . a nice uncle or something."

In so many ways, she was a wise soul, and in others it surprised Sal how innocent she could sometimes be.

"Where's Vince?"

"Safe. Maria knows what's going on and he's with her. I can't run away from this or it would never end. They can go somewhere and wait it out. Vince didn't want to go, but Nick actually convinced him. They met for just a few minutes, but I could tell Vince liked him."

Sal wasn't thrilled to hear that but he could see how it would happen. Though it bothered him a little, Fattelli had a certain presence someone Vince's age might admire.

"That's good under the circumstances." Sal puffed out a breath. "Carre's going to be prepared. First of all, he's always armed under those silk suits. Second, I bet he realizes you'll eventually figure it out. Have you ever noticed he's never alone? He has a driver, a valet, a personal assistant, and so on. All of them do double duty as bodyguards."

Reign stared at him. "How do you know all this and I don't? He and I are in the same industry."

"My father told me when I got my CPA and Carre approached me to handle his taxes. My father's advice was to only accept if I was willing to do whatever the man wanted. That the manicure and bonhomie and designer job did not mean Carre wasn't a very dangerous man." Sal still remembered that conversation, because his father usually let him make his own mistakes. He'd heeded the warning too, and told Joey that his client list was full. "My father rarely gives advice. I took that conversation to heart. Tax evasion has put many a man, and woman for that matter, in prison. The IRS gets real picky about it."

"I've heard that." At least a glimmer of humor showed in her eyes. Reign sat back and adjusted her skirt. "So you decided to become a lawyer instead."

It was a very nice view and he admired it for a moment before he said, "The law is open to interpretation, especially trial law. A tax form is not. It's—"

The skylight in the kitchen shattered.

Sal realized what had happened because from his chair, he could see the cascade of glass, like a crystal fountain, falling to the floor. It took one paralyzed moment before he could move, and by then Reign was already off the couch, grabbing his arm. "Not out the front door," she said in his ear loud enough he could hear it over the barrage of gunfire hitting the cabinets and marble counters. "That's what they want."

Smart girl. "Loft bedroom," he managed to gasp, because it did hurt to run. "We'll be trapped, but it is a defendable position."

"Gun?" Her arm was around his waist and it was uncomfortable, but then again, it helped him move faster.

"More than one," he said through his teeth as they went up the stairs. "I'm carrying my Glock. I've got a .38 up there in a drawer."

"Good, I want to be a part of this. Where is it? And tell me it's loaded."

"Of course. Armoire. Bottom." He really didn't realize how sore he still was, but Sal drew his weapon and positioned himself at the top of the railing so he had a very clear view of the room below. "Take the safety off."

"I know how to handle a gun." Reign joined him, kneeling in her flared skirt, and held the weapon steadily. She added succinctly, "My father taught me, and ask anyone, he's damned good. He made me practice with him and I gradually realized as I got older he wanted me to be able to protect myself. Well, guess what, I can. I hope they try it. I'm getting very tired of this shit. It's making me want to shoot someone."

Sal had to admire the steadiness of Reign's hands. He was outwardly calm but inwardly shaken, mostly because he was worried for her safety. Two men came into view down below in the living room, and the invaders had automatic weapons, and Reign and Sal certainly did not.

*Shit.*

It wasn't like there were a lot of places to go. They would have to come up the stairs to get a clear shot, and except for the sheer volume of ammunition the opposition had, maybe they could deal with this long enough for reinforcements to arrive.

"You get the blond," Sal said on a low whisper. "It's going to take them about two minutes to figure out where we are. I'll aim for the dark-haired asshole. Got it? We don't have much time to discuss this. If they start shooting, we're dead."

"Got it." She moved, lifting up, which made her more of a target, but she was shorter and he understood a clear view was important.

Then one of the men swung around and she fired. So did he.

She must have hit her target because he went down, cursing and raising his weapon. Sal grabbed her and sent her sprawling as a spray of gunfire battered the railings of the loft and took out two windows. Now he was the one swearing and crawling to relative safety, the thick artistic part of the banister at the top of the stairs offering at least some cover. "Stand up and I'll shoot you myself," he said on a hiss. "Let me handle it, unless you have to do it because I'm dead."

His ears were ringing and it hurt like hell to get to his knees, but one of the men was still moving and . . .

Reign completely disobeyed him.

She stood up and fired her weapon again.

Game over. She was a very good shot.

Both of the would-be assassins now seemed to be down amidst the mess of what once was a beautiful living space. Leaning weakly against the top of the stairs, Sal said, "You know, Reign, I think Fattelli has his hands full with you. Serves the bastard right."

# TWENTY-FOUR

Nick realized he was walking into a mine-field.

There was a reason he knew Carre. The man had connections everywhere, and Nick had cultivated the introduction with the sole purpose of being able to have a friend that might be helpful.

Some friend.

Carre's Manhattan office was much more elaborate than Reign's. A corner window, mahogany desk, and if Nick had to call it, the young secretary that had shown him in did more than just take messages.

"Fattelli." Carre rose and offered his hand. "So good to see you. Have a seat."

The shake was brief, but then again, Nick wasn't sure just how this was going to play. He'd seen that wary look in a man's eyes before. "Joey. How are you?"

"Good. Drink?"

"Uhm, no, but thanks."

"Then I repeat, have a seat." Carre waved a hand.

The chair Nick settled into was leather, soft and comfortable, but he was hardly relaxed. Just to make sure, he'd picked a chair with a clear view of the door.

Carre gazed at him expectantly.

Up to him to start the conversation. He got it. No problem. "I'm here because of Reign."

"Grazi?"

"You know someone else named Reign? That surprises me."

"No, can't say that I do." Joey Carre's smile was brief and brittle. "You think I took out the hit?"

"Now . . . *that* is an interesting conclusion and a way to get right to the point. You know there's a hit. Did you?"

"You think I'd admit to something like that?"

"I think you might arrange something like that, or apparently you've heard about it." Nick smiled back. "And that wasn't a denial."

"It wasn't, was it?"

Nick swore softly, "You son of a bitch."

"My mother was actually a pretty nice lady. My father, on the other hand, was an ass." Carre looked unmoved. "You know, the moment I saw you spot Reign at that party, I knew you were going to get involved in this, but hardly the way I wanted. I told Carlos you'd seen his face, he'd better take you out."

"Why didn't you just send him after her in the first place?"

"He didn't do women. Not because he was morally opposed or anything—I'm fairly sure he would not have understood the word 'moral'—but because he was superstitious as hell. Thought his grandmother might curse him if he killed a woman."

"So you sent him after me?" Reign had been right on that score.

"Let's just say when you left together, I assumed from the vibe I was getting that the two of you might end up in her bedroom. She's not promiscuous, but she isn't a nun either. Modern kind of female, and she liked you. After her breakup with Ariano, she's been pretty reclusive." Carre opened a drawer in his desk. Nick knew exactly why. "Her and Ariano? That's why you're here? I'm kind of surprised, given your attachment to the lady, that you left them together."

He didn't like the sound of it. "So you already know where she is?"

"Oh yeah." Carre picked up a pen, but one hand was invisible. "She did a pretty good job with her son and her sister, but I'll find them eventually. Reign and Ariano are already dead, you know. I got a text. It said, 'The party is over.'"

It might not have even been what he said, it was the way he said it. Nick could swear he felt the exact same way he did the day he got the news his sister had been killed. Cold, lethal, the world coming into vivid focus, like a brilliant sunset. "*What?*"

The other man raised his gaze. "About five minutes ago. You shouldn't have left her alone."

There was no doubt Nick was finding it hard to

swallow, much less think. "You're bluffing. And I didn't leave her alone."

"Ariano isn't on his A-game now, is he? Might be those two bullets he took recently. Shame about that. I think it was a case of mistaken identity or you wouldn't be standing here today."

So . . . they knew where she was. Carre was trying to rattle him. The fucker didn't realize it had the opposite effect. He'd wipe that smug look off his face with a bullet. No one could do it better, or for a better cause: to rid the world of an unwanted waste of human cells. All Reign had done to the man was shown more talent in her profession.

Nick said coolly, "His family will run over you like a bulldozer."

"That's my problem, and besides, his family will blame hers. Don't stand up, Fattelli. You'd lose."

Like hell he would. Reign wasn't dead either. He would feel it if she was, or so he assured himself. Maybe it was a superstitious Sicilian belief, but he felt their souls were somehow connected and she was *not* dead.

But Carre would be.

When he'd walked in he'd known he would be outgunned. Only one of him, and Carre was intelligent enough to know if he showed up there might be a confrontation. Nick had to wonder how many guns but really didn't care. He hadn't been so focused since he'd heard about Catherine, and maybe he was a little like his father. If someone deserved to die, they should.

So he stood and said calmly, "Let's go."

"Your meaning?"

"Go ahead. Pull on me. I know you have your hand on a gun. Try it."

The asshole had absolutely no idea how resolute he was.

Or how good he was.

Carre said on a rasp, "You won't walk out of here."

"Neither will you. And as you just said, that's my problem."

It wasn't like he was unprepared.

Carre made the mistake of moving.

Nick had two guns on him, one in the shoulder holster but also one tucked behind his jacket in his pants, easier to reach in a swift, decisive moment. Nick was faster—caught him in the chest with the first shot—and the other man's shot went high, maybe brushing Nick's arm, he couldn't be sure, but he fired again and then Carre was down, sliding out of his chair. . . .

The man had a surprised expression, and it was a very satisfying moment when he went sprawling on the expensive rug, bleeding everywhere.

One down.

Nick fell to the floor as the door burst open, and then he rolled, taking out the first man who came charging in—never a good idea to be first in. The second one was more cautious, just a glimpse of his shadow in the doorway, and Nick called out, "Carre's dead. No paycheck. Back off. Give me a show of empty hands and I won't kill you."

It had happened so fast he wasn't even breathing hard.

Silence. Nick slid back toward the wall, his gun extended.

After a minute, he saw someone set down a gun in the doorway. A voice said, "Look, let me and Joyce just get out of here, okay? You get to deal with the cops. My weapon has my fingerprints on it but it hasn't been fired, so you own those two dead bodies. I bet you'll hear sirens in about two seconds. There are other offices in this building."

Yes, he was bleeding, which meant he was at least nicked a little in the arm. Nick could feel the blood starting to soak his sleeve but adrenaline was an anesthetic. "Deal."

"Never liked working for Carre all that much anyway." The man muttered the words and a moment later the door to the reception area closed.

Fine. *Good.* How to leave the building without a lot of questions was an interesting dilemma, especially since he was bleeding, but he'd never been slow about thinking on his feet. Nick got up, not trusting anything or anyone, but the office outside was deserted. The secretary had even left her cup of coffee still steaming on her desk.

He could only think of one thing.

God, he was worried about Reign. . . . It couldn't be true. . . . It *wasn't.*

Being alone was a familiar friend. He was used to being alone. As he walked swiftly down the hall-way to the stairs, rather than taking the elevator, he reflected that alone was more comfortable, because at the moment, he was frantic.

He called the burner phone he'd given her. Carre was playing him, maybe. . . .

"Hello."

Her voice. He was so relieved he slipped on the stairs and almost went down. It could be that he was bleeding more than he'd thought at first. There was a certain weakness that might be relief but also might be blood loss. "You're okay?"

"Uhm, kind of. Sal and I might be arrested. It seems fifty-fifty at this point. Our family names and this intruder thing happening so often isn't winning our argument. They'd love to arrest someone and the others involved seem to be dead."

But she *was* alive.

Blood dripped from his sleeve in a crimson stream. "I might be arrested too. But Carre feels a lot worse. Actually, let me rephrase, he doesn't feel anything."

"Nick!"

He used the handrail, but his palm skidded along it. "Let's find out how good I am. Say, is it possible Sal could call his doctor friend? I might need a little assistance."

"You?"

He heard the clang of the door at the bottom of the stairs and staccato voices issuing orders. Apparently the officers were covering all the bases. "I've got to get the hell out of here. Have I mentioned yet I'm in love with you?"

"I'm coming to get you."

"No, you aren't." There was no doubt there was a trail of blood. Shit. He didn't want Reign arrested too. He told her as he gained the alley through the back exit, "I'm going to call John. Meet me at the church instead?"

"I'm on my way."

The police were in the stairwell now. He could hear their voices.

*Move it.*

Luckily he had left the Bentley around the corner in a parking garage that serviced blocks of offices and stores, and happened to be fairly deserted at this time. He had no illusions, the police could track him, but if he hurried, he might just walk away from this one.

There were times in his life he hadn't cared much if he lived or died, but since meeting Reign, he was gaining a different perspective.

He fumbled in his pocket and pushed a button and the car came to life. Then he made a second call. "I might need a favor."

"Of course." His brother's voice held alarm. "Nick?"

"I won't stay long, but is there a back door where you can meet me and a place where I can wait for my ride? I might need to leave my car at the church for a day or two."

Just in case anyone remembered the Bentley he was currently bleeding all over. It was a pretty distinctive car.

"What's wrong?"

"It's nothing major, and I promise you, dad would have approved of this one."

John understood. They were brothers, but also part of a brotherhood they'd known their entire life. "I'll pray for their souls. In the meantime, be careful. I'll be waiting."

Warm night, bright stars, and asphalt.

At the end of the day, Reign was left with sitting on the curb outside, as Sal's new doctor girlfriend—or so it seemed—patched Nick up inside the apartment.

At least, if there was a good result to all of this, there was someone to help.

Sal, perched next to her, said with very Italian logic, "That was a good call on his part to ask for Jennifer. Do you and I know how to stitch up another human being? He would have had to go to the hospital, and it didn't seem like something he wanted to do."

Of course not. Then he'd have to explain how he got shot in the first place, and he left the scene deliberately to avoid the police. If Reign had to call it, she'd bet that there was already a request at all the area hospitals to watch for a gunshot victim. Nick had admitted he'd left a trail of blood.

Reign glanced over. Jennifer, was it? First names? She actually was pleased. It said something already that Dr. Altea would come to help if Sal called. Not to mention he obviously had her private number.

Sal looked wiped out again. Who could blame him? She had to ask, "Will she report? I have no idea yet what Nick left behind, but I doubt it was pretty."

"She knows nothing about that and has made it clear she doesn't want to know. I don't think you and I know much about it either. He was shot. That's what I said on the phone and she sure could tell once he got here."

"Joey is dead."

"Oh hell, yes. All over the news." Sal looked a little pale in the streetlight from the parking lot, but not repentant. "I can't believe no one managed to take out Carre before this, but if Fattelli took care of it, maybe he and I could be friends after all."

"This possessive male crap annoys me."

"Get used to it. I think probably Fattelli is pretty good at it. That's my cue to go. Here he comes. Try to be nice. He just took a bullet. I can say with some authority it isn't the most pleasant experience. At least his only went through the upper part of his arm."

"You ask *me* to be nice?"

Sal kissed her. It was brief, just a touch of their lips. "We make a great team, but you aren't still a member." He let go of her hand. "Our last play together was pretty good, though, huh?"

He stood and left. The parking lot smelled faintly of urine, and insects circled the lights, and she really wished she'd bothered to bring down her wine, but maybe the police tape was part of the problem. The neighbors had called in the sound of gunfire.

Sal was replaced by Nick, who sank down on the sidewalk next to her and touched her cheek. "Hey."

Reign looked over. "You look like shit."

She didn't really mean it. He looked fabulous because he was still alive, but his shirt was covered in dried blood and his hair was disheveled and she doubted she looked any better.

"Fuck, the doctor gave me a shot." He rubbed his shoulder but then winced. "I can take the stitching part. . . . I did it without anesthetic. Could she have told me the shot was not optional?"

Reign laughed. "You know we live to torture you, right?"

He took her hand and entwined their fingers. "I do. Women were born to torture men, I get it. Tell me what happened?"

"You did warn they might be coming. But through the skylight? Luckily, Sal wasn't all that surprised. Going upstairs was a very good idea, and we both seem to be good shots. It wasn't luck, really."

"Carre said he got a text you both were dead."

Oh, he had. She'd personally taken the cell phone from one of the men, scrolled through his number directory, and sent it herself. Reign smiled grimly. "That was from me."

"I assume the police took the guns. They'll be able to tell from ballistics."

The interrogation hadn't been all that fun. "The only reason we aren't at the police station is that in a roundabout way they said both of those men were under surveillance for some reason that was not shared with us, and the detectives saw them breaking in. Too little, too late, to really help us, but whatever it was those bastards were supposed to have done, it seems glaringly obvious it might involve contract hits. Otherwise there's no way the cops would have left here without carting us along."

This particular evening, it had been a good thing the police officers were there, even if it was after the fact. Since the incident at her home had involved a similar problem, they'd believed her too.

She tightened her fingers around Nick's. "So it's over?"

He gazed at her with those beautiful blue eyes. "I think so." There was a pause. Then he said, "You did hear me on the phone, right?"

She had. It had been a mistake to go talk to John. Now she understood Nick better, and it made her . . . vulnerable. Worse, she was afraid it made them *both* vulnerable.

"You do realize that you are complicating what seemed to be a mutually satisfying sexual relationship."

"My fault, is it?" He touched her cheek. "You love your son. You love your sister. You love your father, I saw it. You even love Sal, but you aren't right for each other. Isn't there room for one more?"

He had a very good point.

# EPILOGUE

*Italy, eight months later*

That was one hell of a nice wedding." Nick adjusted his sunglasses. "I'm going to say the Ariano family knows exactly how to do it right."

It *had* been a pretty dazzling event.

Next to him on the beach, Reign tilted her head back, the warmth of the sun welcome. "I know I was only invited because they were delighted that Sal was marrying someone other than a Grazi, but I'm okay with that. I actually think our families might have a truce going on."

"True. He married a respectable doctor instead of—"

Reign rolled over on her towel and smacked his bare chest. "Watch it, Fattelli."

He pretended it actually hurt. "Hey. I was going to say the sexiest fashion designer in the world. Her wedding dress was really pretty. Sal was certainly impressed by it from his expression."

That was true. Jennifer had been a very beautiful bride, and Reign had a poignant happiness that Sal had moved on. He was over her and in love with someone else, but then again, she really wished him the best.

And now she and Nick were having a much-needed vacation. The design line was a dream, but a lot of work. Not to mention her empty house, now that Vince was busy with classes and his new friends.

Italy had been a great idea.

The water was a perfect aquamarine and the breeze warm. . . .

"By the way, I love the bathing suit." Nick ran a finger along the edge of her top. "You look hot."

She smiled. He didn't look so bad himself, tanned and muscular. "Good save." She said it dryly, and then added, "I checked the weather on my phone. It's raining in New York."

He reached over and pulled her on top of him in one smooth movement so they were face to face. "This is nice, I agree, but even if we were there, I'd just suggest we spend all afternoon in bed. Kiss me, Ms. Reign Supreme."

She did, long and slow and heated. Mingled breath, brushing tongues; definitely a scorching lover's kiss. "I think we'd better cool it down," she said when she lifted her head and saw a couple walking by smile as they watched them, the man saying something to make the woman laugh. "It seems to me you might have an embarrassing walk back up to the hotel. Swim trunks don't do much to hide your current state of enthusiasm for my company."

"I have a *lot* of enthusiasm for your company," he responded, and audaciously squeezed her ass.

"The feeling is mutual." She smoothed back his hair. "You know me, I like playing with fire."